The World of Hamth

Book 1
The Accidental Cleric

By D.H. Austin

Introduction

Take the road northwest out of Hasgill. You know the little town on the Dior River where it turns south and becomes Lake Porr Triel. It is a good wide road, rising and falling along the rolling hills of the western frontier lands of the country of Goralda in the disputed territories northeast of Holdandun. You will be headed toward the Evernye River. It might take you a few days, or less if you can afford a coach or horse. When you reach the Evernye Crossing go over the bridge and turn to the right there is a village just ahead, up the road a mile or so, on the left. The village is called Rainwash.

Part 1 Prolog

It happens, occasionally, as everyone in the village knows. Wild animals from the mountains to the north stray into the fields and even at times into the village square.

Saxton Brintel, the shire reeve of the township of North Dolwanner, lived in the village of Rainwash. His home was a small cottage close to the village well. His neighbors to the right, the Falloners, and to the left Baantrine the potter, stood this morning on the little porch of Saxton's cottage and pounded upon his door.

"Who on Hamth could that be?" Saxton's wife, Eribeth, said as she slipped her legs from under the blankets of the bed and sat up. As she shuffled her feet next to the bed trying to get into a pair of worn slippers her husband drew the blankets up under his nose.

"Tell the fools that they can come around after breakfast," Saxton grumbled.

Eribeth, a lovely woman with short brown hair and bright green eyes, was popular among all the families of the village. She was known for miles around for her apple pies, crumbled berry pudding, and patience with children. She walked around the bed to her husband's side and dropped her fist onto the top of his balding head with a thump.

"Get up Saxton! If you make me answer the door one more time this week before I've had my tea there'll be no baking in this house for the rest of the summer."

"Oh for…" Saxton went on making incoherent noises and flung his arms and legs about wildly throwing off his bed covers as he got to his feet. He stood in front of his wife, grabbed her around the waist and lifted her off of the floor.

Eribeth squealed. Her abrupt outburst turned into a trill of giggles as her husband nuzzled his rough, unshaved chin into the soft flesh of her neck above her shoulder.

"No baking," he said. "Go home to your mother then. You're of no more use to this man." His playful affection and tender embrace reminded her why she loved him so much.

The sound of the pounding upon his cottage door drained away the charm of the moment.

Saxton set his wife down, kissed her, even nipped at her for a moment or two. Then he took his soft felt hat from the table by the bed, picked up his trousers from the floor where he had left them the night before and went into the small main room of his cottage looking for his boots and socks.
Eribeth let out a sigh and fell back onto the bed saying, "Tell them if they come back in an hour I'll make biscuits."

The cottage was smaller than those of his neighbors, with only three rooms, a bedroom, main room and very large kitchen with a dining table and two chairs. The main room had a small low table with two wooden chairs and a padded and upholstered bench given to Eribeth when she was married. The bench came from her grandmother's house in Sorawinth. Eribeth had fallen asleep on the bench many times when she was a little girl, and her grandmother had always said that when Eribeth had her first home it would be given to her. She had always loved the covering of the seat of the bench. It was a soft heavy blanket like cloth in a checkered pattern, a patchwork of blue and green squares set on a bright yellow backing material, durable, even if it appeared a bit worn when the light came through the windows on the cottage wall that faced south. There was a cabinet, with a small imported piece of mirrored glass above a set of shelves for displaying Eribeth's fine cups and plates, and next to that sat a metal stove, not very large, with a steel kettle resting on the top. All these things were kept free from dust, and the whole of the place was tidy. It wasn't much, but it was comfortable.

Saxton found his boots, with his socks stuffed down into them, near the stove. With one hand he gathered them up while with the other he opened the small door of the stove to see if any trace of fire still lingered from the night before. It was cold, as the fire had long ago gone out, but some small chips of wood still remained. He looked on the top shelf of the cabinet for a match, found one, struck it on the stove pipe and tossed it through the open door onto the mostly burned out pile. Leaving the stove door open, to let the burgeoning fire breathe, he pulled one of the wooden chairs from the low table, and sat down. Once again the pounding on the door sounded. He put on his socks and shoes as quickly as he could, and asked his wife to get a few more pieces of wood for the fire.

Eribeth had dressed in a pale green summer dress and came to the doorway between the bedroom and the main room. Speaking a few strange eldritch words, she cast a spell that lifted a few pieces of wood from the stack in the kitchen and directed them with a gentle sweeping motion of her hand into the stove. Saxton closed the stove door as he rose from the chair and went to the door to see what was the matter.

Part 2

"Good morning sheriff," Mort Falloner said as Saxton opened his front door.

The Falloners were a middle aged couple, nearly forty years old. Mort was a tall man with a medium build. He had been a hired laborer when he was young, and he was a man in good shape for his age. Like most of the men in this part of Goralda he was losing the hair on the top of his head, but it had not begun to turn grey at the sides, like Saxton's. The man had a pleasant face, and Saxton had always liked him.

Saxton's relationship to Mort's wife, Agnes, was a different story. Agnes Falloner was a short heavy woman, with thick powerful arms, and a neck like a bull. She had been beautiful in her youth, but always believed that life owed her more than she received. She married Mort, with both families' approval, and settled into a life as a wife and mother, but she was never happy. Maybe it was because she was spoiled as a child. Maybe it was because she often found fault with others and would gladly talk about her findings for as long as a listener could bear, something Saxton had no patience for. What ever it was, Saxton found her difficult. He had always found her company disturbing, even when they were children. Agnes was Saxton's youngest sister.

The families of the village were mostly descended from the regular sort of humans found all across the eastern counties of Goralda, near the coast. They were brown skinned, dark straight-haired folk, usually tall and strong. Over the years these people migrated westward, over the Ostram Mountains, into the lands near Holdandun, home to the dwarven people. The Dwarves of Holdandun had never been kind to these migrating folk, and so in time most of these humans moved northward into a region known as the Baslinor plain.

Saxton's father, Alrin, had come to these lands sixty years ago with twenty families under the protection of Hiran Jarten, Duke of Everlight. The Duke had obtained permission from the Mashikagima Clan of the Holdandun Dwarves for these people to move into the northeastern lands and settle. The first town they established was Hasgill, then Barrow Willow, then Fawn Valley, and finally Rainwash. Saxton and his sisters, Agnes and Anilia, were born in Rainwash, in a cabin that was destroyed in a fire when they were all very young. After that fire Saxton's parents left Rainwarsh and returned to Goralda. Alrin had not been able to breathe very well after that fire and living at the higher elevation of Rainwash was difficult for him.

When Saxton was old enough he left the village and joined the Duke's army where he served with distinction for nine years. Upon returning to the village of Rainwash Saxton fell in love with Eribeth and married her. Soon after that the Duke received a

charter to establish a township in the lands settled
by these families. Saxton, who was the highest
ranking man in the Duke's service in the township,
was made Shire Reeve (or protector of the peace) in
the township (or shire as some called it in the old
language). As protector of the shire, and the Dukes
representative, Saxton had at first thought he would
be acting as a soldier for the rest of his life, but
being Sire Reeve (or sheriff as the term was said by
the villagers who tended to mix the sounds of the
Goraldun and Holdandun languages into one) really
only meant answering to the complaints of his
neighbors and trying to soothe peoples nerves.

The Falloners, as a couple, were good neighbors.
Having his sister a few fields away wasn't always
as bad as he imagined it would be.

Living closer, just a few dozen yards away was the
potter Baantrine Yasgotomi, a dwarven fellow with
a calm temper and quite disposition. Baantrine often
burned slow fires in the kilns he used to finishes his
wares and he was particular about the types of
wood, and other fuels he burned, claiming it all to
be critical to the perfection of the finish on his
wares. Often these fires produced low hanging
clouds of smoke with a foul odor, but not this
morning. Saxton's home was between the two and
he hadn't noticed anything in the air that may have
troubled his in-laws.

"Good morning folks, good morning Ba'antre," Saxton said having difficulty pronouncing the dwarf's name.

Baantrine bowed at the waist, placing his hands on his stomach as he did, as was the custom of his people and said, "Ashiko Nakomo'oa1, pleasant rising Sheriff-san."

"What brings you good folk to my porch?" Saxton said as he sat down on a small stool near the door and began putting on his hard leather boots. "Surely you ain't come to breakfast. There's nothing out of the oven this early. I suppose I could fetch some cheese, or maybe some turnips from the bin if you're that hungry," he finished saying and chuckled lightly.

"It's come back," Agnes said folding her thick arms across her chest. "You seen what it did the days a fore when it were loose ne'er the Tasnet's place. It's come back and is right over by the well. There ain't none of us can get water this morn."

Before Saxton could ask his sister if she was talking about the unicorn that was loose in the village a few days earlier, Baantrine began speaking excitedly. The dwarf was about four feet tall, heavy built, like his kind, and with a thick head of silky yellow hair wound up into a complex knot on the top of his head. The dwarf was not the type to get aggravated easily and as his temper rose his face, pale naturally, began to flush red.

"I am find damaging of many piece of Onorisha this morning," Baantrine said speaking Goraldun with trouble. "Many turned to ground stacks. Plates, cups," he began ticking off on his short fingers the losses he suffered and saying the words in a short forceful way, "Bowls large, Bowls small. In all counting thirty five Onorisha Masishune, thirty five finished items in same pattern for market. Losing hundred maybe three hundred coin in goods."
Saxton had learned the Holdandun language, well enough for a soldier's purposes, when serving in the Duke's army. He knew he never managed it very well, and he respected, even admired the dwarf for learning as much of the Goraldun language as he had just from living in the village these few years.

As it was, even though Baantrine had an incomplete grasp of the language, the sound of the anger in his voice was unmistakable. His anger came from the presence of a creature he could only see as a nuisance.

A few days ago a young unicorn had wandered into the village. Frightened and confused by the buildings and fences, the poor animal had caused considerable damage, knocking over carts, and braking down fences. Saxton had found the animal running back and forth along the irrigation canal near the Tasnet farm trying to find a place not so muddy that it could climb out and escape.

Saxton had never been close to one of these animals before. He had seen only a few in his life, mostly to the east in the wooded areas close to the mountain passes. After several hours of shooing and waving a table cloth at the animal he finally managed to chase it out of town to the south toward the river. Later when he had sat down to tell his wife about the events, he made no effort to hide his belief that the unicorn was far dumber than the horse and a thoroughly useless beast as far as he could tell.

Now that the thing had wandered back into town he was certain his suspicions were true. "All right I'll do what I can to get rid of it, and this time I'll keep it going as far as I can till I have to turn back before the sun goes down. I'm sorry for the damages to your wares Ban," Saxton said, choosing a nickname for the dwarf he understood the fellow was not offended by.

"You kill it this time. Not run out of village. You kill it," Baantrine said angrily making a chopping motion with his right hand down upon his left palm.

Saxton looked toward his in-laws to see what kind of reaction they would have to the dwarf's outburst.

For a long while many in the village had been uneasy with the dwarf after he had moved here with his family. Most Goralduns have no first hand experience with the dwarven people. Most have no understanding of their culture, their ways at all, and too many Goralduns believed every story they ever heard about the border wars between the countries of Goralda and Holdandun. The villagers were uneasy with Baantrine, not really afraid, but skeptical, and cautious around him. Sometimes Saxton wondered how they would feel if something, or someone, actually dangerous ever came to town, one of the barbarian elves perhaps, from the Three Rivers Region. Now that would be a day to remember.

Agnes was nodding her approval of the dwarf's idea to kill the unicorn, whereas Mort looked uneasy and scratched at the back of his head with one hand.

"I don't want to have to do that Ban. It's only a poor dumb animal. I've heard they're cold hard to train, like the Crown's Wearer they are, all wild and ill tempered," Saxton said watching his sister's frown of disapproval grow.

"That thing might kill someone in the village Saxton," Agnes said. "You already tried to drive it away, and it came back. I say its done had a good deed done for'n it. What if the thing is diseased, rabid or something? I agree with the potter. Kill it. You still have that bow and spear from the Duke. It shouldn't be any trouble for you."

Saxton stared hard at his sister, wondering when she grew to be so callous, but in the end he knew she had a valid point.

"All right I'll get my things. You folks please try not to get close to it, but could you go around and warn everyone else to stay inside I don't want to scare the thing into doing something bad."

Eribeth had come to the door and listened to the last of the conversation and then placed one hand on her husband's shoulder as she said, "It doesn't know bad, Saxton. It doesn't know good. It is an animal. It just is. The gods of good and evil don't torture the unintelligent with matters they cannot understand. If you are going to kill this thing you can't let yourself start thinking you are doing some good to prevent some evil. If my brother were here he would explain it better than I can, but I know that that kind of thinking leads down dangerous roads. If you kill it, it is only because its life has placed burdens upon another's and taking a life for that reason comes from the mind of chaos, and evil, not of law and good."

Agnes took her husband's arm and said coldly, "Come on Mort. That woman has put the bug in his ear and he won't listen to anyone else now." She stepped off of the porch and dragged her husband with her as she stormed off.

"You kill monster? You kill it and it not come back again. Is only way," Baantrine said holding his hands out to his sides pleading with Saxton.

Saxton looked to his wife, and then to the dwarf. "I'll try to do whatever I have to do to make sure it doesn't come back Ban. For now if you would please go warn the others like I asked that would be a great help. I have some gold given to me by the Duke in case of claims like yours, and I will write to the Duke to explain why I decided to compensate you. Honey," Saxton said to his wife, "Please get two three-weights and give them to Ban before he leaves," he turned back to the dwarf and said, "A three-weight is equal to one hundred coins silver. I can give you two for your losses, but no more, and the Duke may disagree and if he does we will work out another settlement, but take it now and be careful. Maybe you can build a fence around your place to keep animals out."

Saxton went back into his home to gather the things he needed as his wife went to the kitchen saying, "Wait there Baantrine. I'll be right back."

Part 3 The Accidental Cleric

A year later Hiram Whales received a letter from his sister Eribeth.

The letter told how Saxton, her husband, had died. He had burned to death in a fire no one had witnessed, and that no one could explain. Just days before, he had killed a unicorn that had wandered into the village. Eribeth explained that since that time many other strange accidents and misfortunes had fallen on villagers living in Rainwash. The letter went on for several pages explaining strange effects witnessed by villagers, and asking Hiram for his interpretation of the phenomena. The letter was dated over four months ago even though it normally took only two months for a letter to travel from western Goralda to Las Rotavas in Liegridan, where Hiram lived. His sister had ended the letter with a plea. She begged for him to ask for leave from his holy orders and to travel to Rainwash to help investigate the bizarre things going on.

Eribeth had never asked him for anything, ever. This gave Hiram a feeling he didn't understand. He didn't know if it was a good feeling or a bad one. She was nine years older than Hiram. When Hiram was twelve, and was selected for the priesthood, his family used the money given to them by The Church to make the trip to Rainwash in the hopes of establishing a large farm. Hiram's natural talents and keen memory were highly regarded, and for him, a man no less, to be selected for the religious training offered by The Church was a tremendous honor for his family. Still, he had missed them, terribly at first, but had found the challenges and great kindness of the Sisters to be rewarding in many ways. He had come to find that the study of the nature of divine magic helped to ease the pain of being separated from them, something he was not expecting.

In the twelve years Hiram had lived in Las Rotavas, maybe twice or three times at most, he had received letters from his father, until his father's death. His father had been well advanced in years before taking a wife as he had been one of those "adventuring wizard" types. He had died of old age just two years after the birth of Hiram's youngest brother Fredthil. That was four years ago. His mother had written only once a year, to ask how Hiram was advancing in his studies, and to tell him all about his relations. But Eribeth had written more often. Sometimes Hiram had received two letters a month from his sister. She had always cheerfully told him the latest gossip, and had exchanged with him questions and discussions of the nature of the differences in the arcane and divine spells.

This letter was nothing like the ones he had ever received from her before. The message of the death of her husband seemed cold and emotionless, but the rest of the letter was intense and filled with specific details about durations of strange fogs and behaviors such as villagers speaking in strange languages or behaving in ways contrary to their usual selves. She spent an entire page detailing the pattern and movement of unusual lights like those produced by the spell *Floating Lights*, but that apparently came into being without any caster. The entire letter was full of great details followed by specific questions, but it was the last question of the letter that troubled him most. It read:

"Memorization and recall being elementary to both the divine and arcane caster, can you tell me if the church has record of the spontaneous casting of divine magic without the aid of relic or item so infused with the necessary rituals and components, arising from an intelligent humanoid creature who appears to be unaware of the magic being controlled, or the desire to control it, but who is proven to be the source of the spell and observed casting with verbal and somatic requirements with no prior study of text or prayer?"

Hiram studied that question for nearly an hour. It was not an uncommon question, for an academic like himself, but as he was officially a cleric (even if he acted more as a researcher of magic spells than anything else). It was a question that The Church might consider blasphemous at the least, and one he was not sure he wanted to try to answer at all.

Hiram sat on a bench outside of the dormitory building where he lived, reading the last question in his sister's letter over and over again. It was a bright sunny day in early spring. The wind was blowing gently in from the sea, to the north, and the gulls were noisy over his head. He did not hear the women approach.

There were five of them. Two of the women were of the clergy, officials of the university, wearing long deep blue colored robes with white belts. They were mature women, orderlies of the hospital and priestesses by rank yet nurses by profession. The other three women wore the uniform of the Sovereign Sisterhood, the military order of The Church. Hiram did not know any of them, but one of them he had seen before and would have recognized immediately, if only he had not been reading at the time.

One of the priestesses cleared her throat and said, "Hiram Whales, you will rise in the presence of the Captain."

Hiram was startled, and fumbled with the pages of his sister's letter as he quickly got to his feet. As soon as he was standing he realized who it was that had come looking for him.

The Captain of the Order of the Blessed Flame, Sisters of Saint Bridgid, Wardens of The Sacred Light of Illumination, her holiness Salindis Marinda Rower, the highest ranking official in The Church's offices of investigation of paranormal activity, and an officer of the Sovereign Sisterhood.

Hiram bowed, a deep bending at his waist, and said, "My apologies Captain, I did not see you approach. Can I be of assistance to The Church in some way I have overlooked?" He was nervous.

Nurses from the hospital were among the most skilled of priestesses. These women would not normally leave the University Hospital and especially would have no reason to come to him for anything. As far as the Sisterhood went, well it was usually never a good thing if one was visited by the Sovereign Sisterhood.

The Captain was by reputation a plain and straight talking woman. Hiram had seen her in the city before, during celebrations and at special events, such as when the city builders had broke ground on a construction project (the new station for the railway system that was moving toward them from the east). He had only ever seen her from a distance, and his opinion had developed that she was a heavy woman of considerable age, but now with her standing right in front of him he realized his mistake.

She was certainly not old, but her hair was bright and silvery, almost white and cut short so that it curled inward below her chin. The stark white of her hair contrasted with the light brown of her skin.

Her face was angelic. She had large brown eyes, a perfectly straight nose, and a small and well proportioned mouth. As for her size, heavy was not the right word at all, massive would be better. The Captain was a good hand's width taller than Hiram, and easily she was double his weight. She was not fat though, her size and her shape seemed to match perfectly. She was thick, in every part of her body from her wrists to her ankles, and the close fitting uniform of the Sisterhood, sized to her perfectly, accentuated her figure. The uniform was dark red, with gold accents, and gold epaulettes. Voluptuous was the word he would use to describe her, and yet he somehow felt even that word was not enough.

From her right hip, slung from a wide green sash around her waist was a long handled, square headed hammer. The handle was polished wood but the head was made from a mirror like metal substance. The war hammer was the symbol of the Sisters of Saint Bridgid. The head of the hammer was etched with the patterns of a blazing fire, and the reflection of the sun on the surface almost made the patterns seem to dance from imaginary heat. On the top of her head sat a tradition short brimmed hat. The hat was flat black with a narrow red band and looked too small for her head.

In comparison, the other two women who were younger and smaller but also wearing the uniform of the Sisterhood, looked childlike.

When the Captain spoke she placed her right hand on the handle of the hammer and looked directly at Hiram, staring into his eyes with her full attention.

"You are Hiram Whales. Your family lives in the northwestern territories of Goralda. I want to, first, apologize to you for this invasion of your privacy, and second to tell you that your services to The Church are, in fact, required,." The Captain then looked from side to side quickly and added, "Are you comfortable talking here about matters concerning your family?"

"Of course, yes this will be fine," Hiram answered.

He resisted his own curiosity to ask why The Church would be interested in his family.

"Good, right," the Captain said and turned to speak to the priestesses. "Thank you. You have been most helpful, but my assistants and I will not need you for anything else. Please express my deepest appreciation to the Reverend Mother for allowing you to take time away from your duties to help us find Mr. Whales." She then made quick hand signals to her assistants who jogged off at a hurried pace to stand fifty yards away from Hiram and the Captain, each taking a stand as if on guard at the ends of the dormitory.

The priestesses bowed, and then began to walk away. As the priestesses reached a place only a few steps away one of them turned her head just slightly, and when Hiram caught her eye she winked slowly.

Part 4

"Can we sit down for a while?" the Captain asked.

Hiram stepped to the end of the bench he had been
sitting on and offered the Captain a seat. Waiting
for her to sit before he did he answered, "Of course
that will be fine."

The Captain smiled and brushed past Hiram, turning
quickly on her heels, with smart military precision
and then checking that her uniform and equipment
were in order, she sat down.

"Hiram please there is no reason to be nervous you
are not in any trouble with the Sisters or The
Church," she said as she patted the bench next to
her. "Sit down. I have just a few questions for you,
then maybe a simple request, and then if things go
as I hope they will I have a very large request."

Hiram sat down next to her, but placed the letter
from Eribeth under his right leg as he did. The
Captain was close to him, her right leg touching his
left leg, and he became nervous for altogether new
reasons.

The Captain removed her hat, placing it gently in
her lap, and turned to face Hiram asking him, "How
long have you been a student here at the
University?"

Hiram remembered his protocol and addressed the Captain politely, "I am no longer a student Ma'am. I graduated six years ago. I have been promised an opportunity for a doctoral thesis application review, and hope to begin work on that very soon. Officially I am Assistant to Madame Dorchester, in the office of State Records, but unofficially I do research for many of the teachers here on campus."

"How old are you?" she asked.

"I will be twenty five years old this fall. I came to the city of Las Rotavas when I was twelve. I was a student at the Nineteenth Mission for three years and then was given a scholarship to the University, but all of this is in The Church records."

"You graduated in three years, with a degree in what exactly?"

"Contemporary history, with a minor in Language studies, again this is all…"

"Did you know Sister Lurain at the Nineteenth Mission?"

That question was not something that someone would learn the answer to by examining church records, and caught Hiram a bit off guard.

"Yes of course, she was very kind to me, very kind to everyone. I learned to read in her classes." Hiram was trying to think of what event, what thing about that sister could be connected to him in such a way that it would draw the Office of Paranormal Investigations. Sister Lurain was the kindest of women he had ever known, a demanding disciplinarian, but a genuinely caring soul, a real special person in many ways, but nothing out of the ordinary came to his memory.

"She was very kind to me as well," the Captain said.

"She taught me how to read as well. She died a few years ago, I didn't know if you knew. When I last spoke to her she told me she had always enjoyed the special children she taught, the quick learners, and the difficult ones. She said they both always gave her a challenge. She mentioned one student that was a combination of the two, you. She told me she always hoped you would go far in your life. Do you want to go far in your life Hiram?"

"I'm not sure how to answer that question properly," Hiram said surprised.

The Captain made a slight noise, almost a squeak that came out sounding like, "Humph." The she cleared her throat and said, "I almost expected you to say, 'yes of course', as you seem to use that expression often."

"Hiram," she went on, "I really would enjoy spending more time getting to know you. I think we could be friends. However, I must get down to business and this business has the potential to possibly make you not like me very much. I am going to make a small request from you, but first I want to ask you to tell me if the letter you are sitting on is from your family in Rainwash?"

The tone of the Captain's voice became more serious than it had been, and Hiram knew, well, the consequences of being indirect with an official of the Sisterhood. He also knew that technically the Sisterhood was not a part of The Church proper, that the two were separated by fundamental ideas about the nature of the church authority, and that if complications arose he could almost certainly count on support, if not protection, from The Church should he need it. Yet still he was curious, and had no reason to believe he, or anyone in his family including Eribeth, were in any sort of trouble.

Hiram took the pages from under his leg and showed them to the Captain saying, "The letter is from my sister Eribeth."

The Captain did not take the pages from his hand, but only examined them slightly before saying, "Yes I know. I wanted to see if you trusted me. I am sorry I did not just come right out and tell you I knew at the start. It seems that the things I have heard about you are turning out to be true."

She turned to be facing him more directly and as she did she subconsciously flipped the hair away from her face. Watching her closely, Hiram felt a lump in his throat grow.

Hiram had not been this close, physically to very many women in his life, most of the priestesses were very conservative, and had significant personal boundaries. But this woman was no priestess, nor was she a student, which had an entirely different set of standards keeping distance between him and the opposite sex. In fact this was the first time he had sat this close to a woman almost his own age in over ten years.

"I am feeling that I am making you uncomfortable Hiram," she said as she drew away from him a few inches. "I don't want you to feel awkward, and I need us both to feel we can trust each other. So I will give you permission to ask me a few questions if you'd like, but not too many, and then I will tell you the small favor I need from you."

Hiram was not sure what kinds of questions he would ask the Captain, a member of the Sisterhood, a woman. He thought for just a second and then asked, "How old are you Captain?"

"I am forty one, but I often tell people I am thirty nine, only because at my age I should have reached the rank of Lieutenant Colonel, but I don't really need to go into all the reason why I haven't yet. And please call me Salindis, or Sister Rower if you prefer, we really only use our ranks within the organization and try to emphasize our place as sisters of a common cause when interacting with people outside of our own little structures."

Hiram was struggling to think of another question,
an appropriate question, when the Captain pushed
the hair on the left side of her face behind her ear,
and Hiram suddenly blurted out, "How did you get
such light colored hair?"

The Captain laughed, and leaned forward a bit as
she patted Hiram's hand, which was placed upon
his knee.

"Fair enough, fair enough," she said. "That is an
even longer story than the one about my lack of
promotion, and I really, really do not have time to
tell it to you, but I hope some day I can. I will tell
you this, as a bit of advice, when dealing with
scrolls, spell scrolls, it is never wise to assume, no
matter how talented you think you are, that you can
handle one not appropriate for you. My hair was
once the same color as my eyes, and after that
incident it turned to this," she said holding some of
the locks out away from her head. "Some people
find the contrast of the brown skin and white hair
very unsettling. Is that what is bothering you
Hiram?"

"Um, no. Not at all," Hiram said. "It's very pretty, I
mean very attractive, I mean it looks good on you,
oh I'm sorry I never wanted to seem forward,
especially with you Captain."

"It's not forward at all Hiram. We of the Sisterhood
take very different vows than your priestesses. I am
flattered. Do you have any more questions? But

please take it easy on me," she said with a warm smile.

Hiram didn't hesitate. By now he was desperate to know the details of why she had come to see him.

"What is it you want to ask of me?" he asked.

"I want you to go to Rainwash," she answered.

"Is that all?" Hiram was puzzled. "You just want me to go to the town where my family lives? That seems, if you will forgive me, a bit strange."

"I suppose it does seem strange. It is the small request I mentioned. And let me be clear, I want you to go to Rainwash. It is not on behalf of the Sovereign Sisterhood that I ask this, but me personally, I want you to go. You see right now your superiors, and many other prominent women of The Church, are having a serious discussion about whom, exactly, they are going to send to Rainwash. And send someone they will. They really will have no other alternative, and I imagine they may even send more than just one or two of their own. My order intends to send someone as well."

"Let me tell you now what the bigger request I have for you is. Hiram," she said now taking both of his hands in hers. "Something of tremendous significance is happening in Rainwash. It is my responsibility to send a representative of the Office of Paranormal Activity to Rainwash, and the woman I have in mind for the job is the best I can think of for the task. The Church has agreed to allow my agent to join the representatives who will be going there on behalf of The Church at Ses Theeth. In my vows I am not at all unsure that what The Church determines what must be done will be done, based on the things they are hearing about the goings on in Rainwash, but something my mother told me when I accepted the responsibilities of my post, some ten years ago, keeps going through my mind. Can I tell you what that thing is?"

"Yes, of course," Hiram answered.

"There's that expression you love. My mother told me that sometimes there comes along a person who sees things very differently, very much clearer than you would recognize at first, and when this special person is available to you never, ever let them slip away from you. Keep that person close to you. Make this person your friend, because this might be the only person to tell you what, truly, is the right thing to do, when no other thing makes sense. My mother told me this not exactly in the way I am telling it to you she said it just a bit differently."

Hiram was intently listening to the things the Captain said, and was curious as to what the difference could be, and if it was significant and if that was why she was making a point of telling him.

"What did she say differently?" Hiram asked almost breathlessly.

"Oh something silly really," she said. "You see my mother never actually said 'special person' or anything cryptic like that when she told me this thing. She was a bit more specific and actually said it was you, Hiram Whales. You knew my mother as Sister Lurain. My mother had a very high opinion of you, and often would tell me that I should be watching you more closely. Hiram, The Church is going to be selecting people to go to Rainwash. I want you to go to Rainwash, but if you go as the representative of The Church I won't feel so guilty about asking you to go, for myself. If you can get permission to go to Ses Theeth, apply to be reviewed as a candidate for this assignment, I can promise you that the woman I send with you from my organization will protect your life with her very own, and I am just going to come right out and tell you that there is a terrible level of danger involved that as of now we do not completely understand. I can brief you on all the details we know, but I guess what I want to know is if you will do the small thing I am asking, and if you will consider doing the bigger thing I will be asking."

Hiram thought hard about what the Captain was asking. He had expected to spend the next two years preparing his Doctoral thesis. He never imagined he would have this kind of thing drop into his lap. The Captain was the head of one of The Church's top intelligence organizations, and most certainly knew everything there was to know about him, and still was it even possible she could know his innermost thoughts. Hiram was a scholar, and a timid man by all accounts, but Hiram was also a brother to a troubled sister, and had always made excuses for never taking the time to visit Eribeth. Now Eribeth seemed to be involved, in some way, with a matter important to The Church, and that made Eribeth important to him on two counts.

Hiram swallowed hard and took a deep breath before saying, "I will ask The Church to consider me for this mission, but Sister Rower can I trust you?"

Part 5

"I want you to trust me," the Captain said. "I don't want to give you the idea that I do not, and if I have I apologize. What is it? Is something troubling you about what I have asked? Do you have more questions about the situation? Because I can tell you as much as I know, but I really think it would be better if you spoke to your superiors first."

Hiram was still holding his sister's letter while the Captain held onto his hands. "Have you all ready read this letter?" He asked.

"No I have not," she answered. "And no one in my organization has either. That it came from your sister was made known to me by the people in your organization. I simply asked if you had, in fact, received any letters from them. Contrary to what you may have heard we don't spy on very many people."

"Something my sister asked me, in this letter, is very peculiar, and potentially damning. I want to share it with you, but I need to know that I can trust you will not take action against her until I have had a chance to speak to her in person in order to find out what she really means by asking."

"I promise to make no judgments on the letter until you have spoken to your sister," the Captain said as she released Hiram's hands

"Look here at this," Hiram said sliding closer to her and rifling the pages to bring the last one to the top of the stack. "She asks, right here…" Hiram stopped himself from dictating the words and pushed the letter into the Captain's hands.

She took the page, giving Hiram a curious look, and then bent over the page and began reading. After a brief pause she lifted her head toward the sky and closed her eyes. She let out a breath and said softly, "Then it is true."

"What?" Hiram asked, suspecting he knew what the Captain was thinking. "What is it you think is true?"

"Evidence of spontaneous casting," she said now lowering her head and placing her free hand to her temples rubbing them lightly.

"That is what it would seem like she is suggesting, but I think there is more here than she is telling me," said Hiram.

The Captain stood abruptly, tugged downward on her uniform jacket, and then said, "You should report to your superiors as soon as you are finished. If you need to speak to me again I only ask that we are always clear with each other in what capacity we are speaking." She took a few steps away from Hiram and signaled for her assistants to return to her. The two women recognized the signal immediately and began jogging quickly to rejoin the Captain. "As these events unfold we, you and I, are most certainly going to speak again. We may speak as friends, or we may speak as officials of our organizations. I feel that it will matter significantly that we always understand in which capacity it is."

Hiram stood and gave the Captain a bow of respect saying, "I understand, of course. Sister," he went on, "Can you tell me how quickly The Church will be moving on this matter? Do I have time for some research of my own?"

"I can't be sure," she replied as she began to walk away and continued saying over her shoulder, "The Church is keeping very quiet on this matter, but I can guess that in a week, not more than two, they will be ready to outfit a group to investigate the events in Rainwash. Meanwhile your superior wants to see you right away, and I don't want to be blamed for keeping you longer than necessary."

Hiram hurried after her and when he caught up to her he asked, sounding as stern as he could bring himself to be, "How do you know I am wanted in the office of the University President?"

The Captain stopped and turned saying, "One of the priestesses winked at you very slowly, with her right eye, and unless there has been a change since the last release of interdisciplinary codes and signals, that would mean you are to report to the reverend mother immediately."

Hiram smiled, for the first time, and said, "You know all about the interdisciplinary codes and signals?"

"Of course," the Captain said affecting the same tone and delivery of the phrase as Hiram had so often done. "We know as many of The Church's secrets as they know of ours. It's probably why we all get along so well."

Without warning the Captain leaned in close to Hiram and put her arms around his shoulders and whispered into his ear as she gave him a strong and very friendly hug. "Be careful Hiram," she said. "And always remember the things my mother taught you. Make good choices, give the benefit of the doubt, and love with all of your heart."

Hiram was comforted, and felt special in the embrace of the Captain.

"I will," he replied as she released him from her arms.

He watched the three women of the Sisterhood walked away, toward the road that left the university and led back toward the city center. He arranged the pages of the letter from his sister, placing them in proper order and ensuring all the pages were aligned correctly with each other, folded them twice into a neat little square, and then placed the pages into his inside vest pocket.

He checked his own garments. He was wearing a casual suit, not something he would wear if teaching, but something more than just a tunic and pants. It was what he might wear if he were going into town for a bit of shopping. He decided the suit was not proper enough for an audience with the reverend mother.

"The charcoal suit with grey tie and the polished shoes I think," he said to himself as he hurried toward his room in the dormitory building behind him.

The doors to each room of the dormitory building faced the courtyard and his room was just a few yards away from the bench where he had been sitting.

He changed quickly, also taking the time to wash his face, just in case, and comb his hair. He had always had trouble with his hair and never really knew how it was supposed to be combed in order for it to lie flat against his head. His hair was thick, very dark, and tended to curl in strange places. He wet down his hair after growing frustrated by not getting anywhere with just the dry comb and when he was satisfied he looked appropriate for an audience with the reverend mother he took his sister's letter from the vest pocket of his other suit and placed it gently in the coat pocket of the jacket he now wore.

The reverend mother was the most highly educated person he had ever met in his entire life. Many foreign dignitaries had visited the university in the years Hiram had been a student, and associate professor, but none of them had come close to possessing the phenomenal scope of knowledge the reverend mother possessed. Her name was Gadilinna Moesteri and she was eighty three years old. She had been both a High Priestess of The Church and in her youth a member of the Sisterhood, something that was not altogether uncommon fifty years ago. She had traveled to as far away as the capital of Anthandra, a city called Byl Roche, over a thousand miles to the east and spent many years in missions across the sea to the south on the jungle coasts of Tradis. She served on The Church's Administrative Council for twelve years before being nominated to a post as Dean of the School of Antiquities here at the University of Las Rotavas of the Blessed River, a place of higher learning established as a cooperative effort between the country of Liegridan and The Church at Ses Theeth.

There was, already, a much larger university on the tip of the Theeth peninsula, at the city of Ses Theeth and she could have gone there, but Her Holiness Mother Moesteri choose to accept the position here and made no secret that she intended to someday rise through the faculty to become head of the entire university. It was whispered that her parents had been born in Las Rotavas and that she had always dreamed of retiring close to her ancestral home.

For over a thousand years the city of Ses Theeth, and the peninsula where it was located, had been treated as an autonomous region whose government was The Church itself. The Church ruled over the everyday lives of almost a million people. Liegridan, the country that was immediately to the east of the Theeth peninsula, was ruled by the Senate of Lieger. The Senate of Lieger was a body of noble men and women descended from ancient houses that once ruled as kings and queens of small, sometimes tiny, kingdoms scattered across the fertile valleys and plains of Liegridan. The whole of Liegridan was three times the area of the Theeth peninsula but its population was just under four hundred thousand. Liegridan was bordered, to the east by the Cyrixtel Mountains, to the south by the river Santi Coslerinos, and to the north by the river Wahl. To the north of the river Wahl were the southern hills of Goralda, and across the river Santi Coslerinos to the south were the marshes of northern Tradis.

Hiram had never been to the city that was the seat of The Church's power in the known world, Ses Theeth. He had never been into the Theeth peninsula for that matter, and he remembered little of his life before he came to Las Rotavas. The thought of traveling abroad, across the Ses Mar to Holdandun or to Tradis, or even out into the great ocean to the west had never appealed to him.

As he walked briskly across the campus toward the office of the university president he began to wonder if he was ready to travel now. He wondered if he was ready to talk about asking to be sent to Ses Theeth for the mission he had just only minutes ago learned about. It occurred to him that he did not know if the reverend mother even knew about the matter in Rainwash. This made him wonder if he was headed toward a confrontation in which he might be asked question for which he did not have the answers.

Hiram was well aware that over the centuries, eight to be exact, there had been varying levels of cooperation and amicability between the priestesses of The Church and the women who belonged to the Sovereign Sisterhood. At times the Sisterhood had been the closest ally of The Church and at other times there had been great divisions between them (none of course greater than the Great Schism, when The Church declared war on the Sisterhood and nearly persecuted them to extinction). However, currently relations were very strong between the two. Missions and orphanages (the primary occupation of the Sovereign Sisterhood) were often staffed by both clerics of The Church and officers of the Sisterhood working in harmony. If the Captain knew what was being planned in Ses Theeth surely the reverend mother knew as well.

Right now Hiram began to ask himself if he was possibly headed into a conflict between the two religious organizations or something worse. Was he going to be the catalyst?

While his mind had pondered these questions Hiram had walked all of the way across the campus of the university. He now found himself standing only a few steps away from the open courtyard of the building that served as the offices and residence of the president of the university, the on campus home of the reverend mother.

The courtyard was a circular area lined all around with narrow free standing columns reaching to ten feet or so in height surrounding a grassy park some fifty yards across with flower gardens and a single central fountain. The fountain had always been one of Hiram's favorite pieces of architecture on the campus. It was a pool twenty five feet in diameter and three feet deep. The low wall surrounding the pool was made of white marble and finished on the top with several benches for comfortable sitting. At the center of the pool was a collection of eight marble statues each in different shapes representing great mammals of the sea. There were three whales, two pinnipeds, one tarodipod, one carpidiped, and one creature he had never been able to identify. These eight statues were made from various marbles, in different colors, and were all nearly the same size (not meant to be in any kind of scale with one another). All were six to eight feet in length and they were clustered, grouped as it were, in a circle around a central column of green marble twelve feet high that was plumbed so that a constant flow of water sprayed out of it and onto the statues. The water was salty. It was supposed to come all the way from the beaches of Casaisis, three quarters of a mile to the north.

Around the courtyard were a dozen or so priestesses of The Church and a few of the non clergy administrators and professors. Hiram could not know why they were gathered, as they were now, typically you never saw more than one or two people lingering around the courtyard.

Telling himself to be very careful about revealing anything the Captain had said to him earlier he began to walk slowly to the left of the fountain crossing the courtyard and making his way toward the large residence style building set close to the columns to the west of the fountain.

Three women approached him. They were moving quickly.

The three women were Alison Mein, Jessily Tocate, and Francine Castenate. All three of them were professors in the university's pre-law undergraduate studies program. Each was a teacher of contract law. They were women in their thirties, all of them, attractive and in good health. He hardly knew them professionally or otherwise. He only knew them by their names and faces because he had delivered volumes of documents to them in his duties.

Alison was in the middle of the three and approached him slightly ahead of the others. She was a short, curly-haired woman with a button nose and a wide smile. She put her left hand on Hiram's chest, stopping him in his attempt to avoid them, and said to him in a hushed voice, "So tell us. Did she ask you to go?"

Hiram was startled. How could they possibly know? His mind raced. Was someone in the university staff scrying on him the whole time? Scrying on the head of a department of the Sovereign Sisterhood? Is that really how The Church operated? Was no one's privacy sacred? His mind filled with these questions.

Very quickly he began to realize that these women were determined to have an answer. He struggled with some idea of how to extricate himself from the situation without betraying the Captain's confidence. He wondered to himself, "Perhaps they don't know anything and it is all just to see what I will say. Either way if I play the fool I may get around the whole issue."

"She might have asked me a few questions," Hiram said, blushing slightly without realizing it.

The three women laughed naturally and loud. Alison took her hand off of Hiram's chest and folder her arms across her own chest. She wore a light cream colored suit and the dark color of her hands stood out against the fabric as she drummed her fingers against her elbows.

"So you're going to play that game?" Alison said. "Very well I'll be direct. Did the Captain of the investigators ask you, Hiram Whales, to be her escort to the annual spring festival dinner to be held at Senator Raimond's estate next week?"

"What?" Hiram stammered completely confused.

"You are such a pig," Alison squealed gleefully as she swatted at Hiram's arm.

Francine moved closer. She was a taller woman, with a very imposing posture, large in front, and typically her face was cold as stone (she had a reputation for being short tempered and impatient with students who tended to make excuses for not being able to keep up with the pace of her lessons). She tipped her head down and peered closely at Hiram's eyes as she said, "Everyone on campus is talking about how she has been going around the place asking every imaginable question about you. She may be a bit older than you but she has certainly got good taste. You can tell people I said that. We all know you are shy and keep to yourself but you had the highest marks in your class and obviously she knows that. Your work ethic is impeccable, and everyone knows when a soldier of the Sisterhood decides to take a husband they choose carefully and thoroughly. So stop being evasive and just tell us yes or no. Did the Captain ask you to be her escort or not?"

Three things bothered Hiram.

He had no idea what this festival they were talking about was. He had no idea people on campus talked about other people's lives in these matters. Most importantly this woman just told him her opinion was that he was an acceptable suitor for one of the most prestigious women in the city. This woman, Francine, had written opinions used to make law in the house of the senate of Liegridan.

His stomach knotted and he tried to speak, "Uhm, she and I talked about my family, and that I knew her mother, but the subject of this festival never came up."

Without even trying Hiram had made tremendous progress in dealing with their curiosity. They all seemed to take his explanation as a good thing.

Alison said, "She has always been a very smart woman, very smart. It makes complete sense that she wouldn't ask you in the first meeting. She obviously needed to see how you'd react to her up close and in person. So tell us. Are you seeing her again? Did you two make any plans? Oh listen to me," she finally broke off her questioning and waved her hand in front of her own face dismissing her own behavior. "How rude am I?" she said with a chuckle. "Don't keep us in the dark Hiram. We know you are going to get a promotion out of this no matter what happens. You deserve it anyway, and when the reverend mother finishes with you I bet you will be cleared to begin your doctorate immediately. Come on ladies lets find somewhere to wait and maybe we can watch."

Alison moved away and the other two women followed. Hiram was curious and had to know what she meant by her last comment.

"What do you mean watch?" he asked.

"Oh I suppose you'll find out anyway as soon as…" Alison could not finish as the third woman, Jessily (who had been silent all along), interrupted her.

"The reverend mother is coming out here to speak with you. Word started spreading around as soon as the Captain asked permission to speak to you privately. I think the reverend mother wants everyone to hear the conversation she is going to have with you. You have no idea how important something like this is for the university, for The Church, for you obviously. Well, for all of us," Jessily's sentences all ran together as she was almost incapable of containing her excitement.

This was a disaster, Hiram thought. How could he broach the subject of a possible heretical event in Rainwash if everyone believed he was going to be discussing the possibility of a date with the Captain?

Just then he noticed, out of the corner of his eye, the door of the house beyond the courtyard opening. A procession began to file out of the door. In the middle of the group of deep blue robed women was the reverend mother. She was being pushed in a large backed wheelchair by Madame Dorchester.

Part 6

Madame Dorchester was not a priestess. Among the university faculty approximately one in ten were not ordained. Madame Dorchester was an older woman, almost sixty. She was short and spry. A woman with an energetic personality and a mind for numbers that was incredible. She had been the keeper of the universities records (some called her the Bookkeeper General) for over twenty years. Hiram had always imagined that Madame Dorchester looked like what his own grandmother might have looked liked. At least he felt she could be anyone's grandmother. It was just the way she looked. Her face was round and a bit pudgy with a small wrinkled chin, puffy checks, and bright hazel colored eyes surrounded by just the right amount of wrinkles. Her hair was a mixture of brown-red and grey that she wore in a bun on the back of her head.

Even before Hiram had earned his degree he had established a professional, and friendly, relationship with Madame Dorchester. There was a synergy about them. She could recall numbers, important as the entire library of the university was cataloged into a ten group set of six digit numbers, and Hiram had a knack for understanding how the works were organized into those sets of numbers (but in honesty he was better at remembering the content of the works and not always the exact iteration of the catalog numbering sequences). Together the two of them could identify, and retrieve, multiple volumes

of obscure scrolls, pages of letters saved from the
universities years of correspondence with The
Church, or any other reference material in typically
under an hour.

No one doubted, ever, that Hiram would be asked to
stay on at the university after he graduated. He was
offered a job as Madame Dorchester's assistant
before he was offered a teaching position. He was
honored to take the job when it was offered.
Besides, it had always been his intention to earn a
doctorate in history and the job was perfect for that
work.

But things, for the last six years, had not gone
exactly as he imagined they would. He expected to
be given his letters of introduction, formal papers
that made it official he was being considered for a
doctoral degree, no latter than one year after
graduation. When he had not received them in three
he considered leaving the university, but Madame
Dorchester begged him to stay. She offered him a
generous increase in salary as a concession. Another
year passed and still there were no letters. The last
two years brought again higher salaries, and a
teaching position, but no letters. At the end of last
year Madame Dorchester confided in him telling
him the truth of the matter. It was understandable if
somewhat difficult to take. He had known all along
that in the history of the university no male had ever
been selected for a doctoral program.

That was simply the way things had been. The Church was not against men becoming priests, not in over five hundred years. Hiram had read literally hundreds of papers on the arguments for inclusion of men in the hierarchy of The Church, and over the centuries many very prominent writers (and at least one Ghedda) had argued for opening up the highest tiers of authority in The Church structure to males. In every case that the matter was brought before the Collective at White Hall the issue did not pass vote. It had never bothered Hiram that of his classmates at the university (and there were over thirty males, three dwarves and even an elf!) he was the only male undergraduate candidate that was granted permission to take the test for priesthood. Those had been some difficult times. He knew, and had been told often, that to dwell on the comments of a few Church women still holding prejudicial opinions was not healthy. No one ever openly challenged him, and many, very many women of The Church, respected him for his sense of duty and humility.

The day Madame Dorchester showed Hiram the letter, from the Councilwoman Secretary of the Collective at White Hall, expressing sadness that the issue of his candidacy for a doctorate had been killed in committee was both painful and encouraging. The letter made it very clear that Hiram's personal records and performance had been reviewed by nearly every member of the Collective and that a poll taken showed that had the issue gone to the floor of the White Hall, been read before the entire Collective Assembly, it would have passed

with a majority but the Council members were
swayed by representatives of the Sovereign
Sisterhood. Most of the Council members had been
Sisters in their youth. The matter ended there, in the
Council, and was never brought before the
Collective.

But Hiram never held a grudge against the Council
or against the Sisterhood. That would just be
childish and wrongheaded. The Sisterhood did not,
ever, act out of prejudice or malice. The Sisterhood
was only acting in the best interest of The Church.
In many ways Hiram could understand their
position. That was how he had been raised, not to
hold opinions based just upon his own feelings or
desires, but on rational and thorough understanding
of things as they were.

He believed, with all his heart, that he would
eventually be granted his letters of introduction. He
believed this because he loved The Church and it
came back to him, now, how very important the
teachings of Sister Lurain had been. He loved The
Church with all his heart.

Seeing Madame Dorchester with the reverend
mother had brought back all of these memories, and
with them the notion that to ask to be included as a
candidate for a mission of such relevance would
almost certainly be the end of his chance at a
doctorate (if he actually were selected). On top of
these troubling thoughts he was still having trouble
wrapping his head around the idea that the reverend

mother wanted to see him because rumors had been going around that he was being courted by the Captain.

The procession of women came toward him. He was deep in thought and before he knew it they were standing right in front of him. When he realized they had come so close he remembered his manners. Hiram bowed, deeply, and said, "It is my honor."

Madame Dorchester maneuvered the wheelchair through the crowd to come right up to Hiram. The reverend mother looked well. She was a small, frail woman. Her legs were wrapped in a white cloth embroidered with blue silk threads in patterns of ocean waves turning over at their crests. Across her arms was folded a blue silk stole and on her head a matching square cap. Her robe, barely recognizable under the other garments, was bright green (the color of the order of Saint Bridgid, of the Sovereign Sisterhood).

The reverend mother slowly lifted her left arm and waved toward a priestess standing toward the back of the procession. The woman came forward. She was a woman Hiram did not recognize. She was short, very short, with light brown almost fair skin and short cut black hair pinned up and back behind her ears. Her head was held downward and Hiram could not make out the details of her face. In her hands the woman carried a stack of sealed letters.

"Hiram Whales," the reverend mother began to say, her voice surprisingly clear and loud for her age. "The honor is this university's, and mine, for it is my privilege to award you these letters of introduction."

Before she could say anything more the whole courtyard erupted in applause. The reverend mother smiled and tried to quiet the noise with gestures but the thunderous clapping continued for over a minute. It was then that Hiram noticed that behind him, while he had been deep in thought, the courtyard had filled up.

Hiram looked around and could not count the number of people who had filled the garden area. It was as though every member of the faculty, and nearly every student, had somehow been quietly nearby waiting for the reverend mother to come out and as he was daydreaming about his past they all had moved in around him.

When the clapping finally stopped the reverend mother continued.

"Hiram Whales," she said, just a little quieter now. "The University of Las Rotavas of the Blessed River takes tremendous pride in this honor. Your exemplary performance as both a student and a priest of The Church has not gone unnoticed. We all have the highest hopes for your future. This great blessing upon you and upon those who have been your teachers, your counselors, and your friends is not better deserved. We all hope you share this blessing not just in the immediate future but for all of the rest of your life. I am personally honored to be the president of the university at this time," the reverend mother lifted her arms and beckoned for Hiram to come closer to her, "Though," she said even more softly, and Hiram began to wonder if she had exhausted her strength. Understanding what the reverend mother was gesturing for him to do Hiram knelt down in front of the wheelchair. The reverend mother leaned forward to hug him around his head saying in almost a whisper, "It may be that I will be forgotten. This thing will not be."

Part 7

When the reverend Mother released Hiram from her hug the applause began again. Hiram took the opportunity of the distracting noise to lean close to her and ask, "I don't understand reverend mother. I thought you wanted to see me for another reason. I haven't prepared any statement. I am so tremendously honored, but I feel I do not have the appropriate words to express myself. What should I say?"

He was surprised to see that the reverend mother, though looking from one person to another in the crowd and waving a slight shake of her hand, heard and responded immediately to his question. Her voice regained some of its strength and was just loud enough for him and only a few around them to hear. "Say thank you, and take the letters," she said.

Hiram realized that the woman with the letters in her hand was still standing quietly next to him with her head bowed and her hands outstretched toward him with the stack of decorated envelopes. He stood and turned towards the woman. He took the letters from her and as he did the stack, which was quiet large, slipped apart. The letters fanned out and almost fell out of the woman's hands. Hiram reached out and tried to catch the letters gathering them together again. That is when he realized that the reason the stack came apart was because the woman was holding the bottom letter tightly with

two of her fingers causing him to have to tug on it
to get her to release it. He didn't notice if anyone
else witnessed the tug of war with the bottom letter
as his gaze had been directed toward the woman's
lowered face. When he tried to pull the letter away
she had lifted her head and he then saw that she was
no woman at all but just a girl. She was just a child
in fact. She couldn't be more than fifteen or sixteen
years old.

Hiram was about to say something when the girl
made a 'shush' sound and he felt the reverend
mother tugging at his arm.

He looked down at the reverend mother and met a
stern gaze. The reverend mother smiled showing her
teeth and said through them trying not to move her
lips, "Say thank you and take the letters."

"Thank you, thank you," he said as the last letter
came free in his hands and then he turned around to
show everyone that he had accepted them. The
applause grew louder.

When he turned back toward the reverend mother
the young girl who had handed him the letters was
gone.

"Reverend mother," Hiram said as the applause
finally died down. He felt that the thing to do was
be direct and ask her specifically about the matter of
his relationship with the Captain. With nearly
everyone on campus in attendance at this moment

any rumors could be squelched and people could be set to right. "About the Captain, Sister Rower of the Sovereign Sisterhood, I was wondering if we could address some possible rumors. There seems to be a story going around that…"

Madame Dorchester came from behind the reverend mother and embraced Hiram saying loudly, "Congratulations Hiram," and then whispered into his ear, "Now is not the best time for that."

But the reverend mother had something of her own to say on the matter. "It would please me greatly if you would accept her offer to be her escort to the spring festival. She is a remarkable and deeply spiritual woman whom I have respected for many years. It only adds to the…" Before she could go on Madame Dorchester leaned over to whisper something into the reverend mother's ear.

There was an exchange of glances between the two women. Hiram did not understand the meaning of the look they exchanged, but it appeared both women were suddenly struggling for something to say.

A voice called from the crowd not far from them, "She hasn't asked him yet," and a series of laughs sprang up around them. It was Alison who had spoken.

Hiram expected the reverend mother, and Madame Dorchester, to be slightly embarrassed but as he

watched their reaction to the laughter he noticed
they weren't listening and instead were still trading
whispers.

"I don't understand reverend mother," Hiram said.
"Has there been some talk of the Captain's
intentions that I should be made aware of?"

The reverend mother pulled at Hiram's sleeve once
again, as she had done earlier, and when he had bent
close to her she said so quietly he almost could not
hear her, "A minor error in communication. Read
the letter as soon as you get to your apartment."
Before Hiram could say anything else the reverend
mother's chair was spun away from him (Madame
Dorchester had moved back behind the wheelchair)
and the procession of people who had come out
with her moved quickly back toward the house.

For the next several minutes the crowd moved in
toward Hiram. Each and every person there wanted
to congratulate him personally. People moved up to
him and either hugged him or shook his hand. It
seemed as though it would go on all through the
afternoon. He had no idea how much time had
actually past when the last of them finally
dispersed.

Hiram hurried back to his apartment, after the
crowd had gone, and laid the stack of letters upon a
dark wooden desk sitting in the corner of his small
one room apartment. He changed clothes, putting
away the nice charcoal suit, and putting on a simple

robe and pair of pants. He sat down at the desk and slid the stack of letters aside until the bottom letter was sat apart by itself. It was in the same large and decorated envelope as the others but it was not addressed. He opened it slowly taking a single heavy sheet of parchment out of it. Unlike the sort of introduction letters he had seen, and cataloged in the universities library, this was an unfolded small heavy piece of yellow paper with light writing in a small script. It was brief and direct:

Hiram,

Two of the letters have been accidentally signed by the wrong individuals. You must bring these letters to my office after evening services. If anyone asks you why you are out simply show them the letters of introduction to professor's Kinier and Graindur. Come directly to my office. You will be followed. Do not take notice of the person following you and do not speak to her. Burn this letter after you understand what must be done.

Prayers Be With You,
 Rubynna Dorchester

His heart pounded in his chest as he read the letter. Hiram could not understand what all of this meant. Earlier, when he had been sitting with the Captain in the warm morning sun, he had not imagined the day would be turned inside out with intrigue. There were too many questions. He tried to organize his thoughts. He began by trying to see how the letter

from his sister, The Church's interest in the events
at Rainwash, the announcement of his candidacy for
a doctorate, and the romantic interests of the
Captain could all be connected. He could not see
how they were, but he kept trying.

He took down a stoneware bowl from a shelf above
his desk and took a match from the desk drawer. He
ignited the note and held it sideways allowing the
flames to engulf the entire document before
dropping it into the bowl where it was soon reduced
to ashes. He had never done anything like this, ever.
He had read accounts of intrigue, and stories of
mysterious doings, but never imagined he would get
caught up in one himself. The mystery at Rainwash
was intriguing, but the mystery of the Captain's
intention was more than that.

A thought came to him. He began to wonder if he
had been too interested, all of his life, in the things
found in books. He had been a good student, a
dedicated teacher, but never a social person. It
wasn't that he deliberately avoided people. He was
always nice and respectful when in the company of
others at either official university events or when in
the city on his own, but it was no secret he preferred
to be alone. He did not try to keep up with the status
of the extra curricular activities sponsored by the
university, the musical performances by the school
orchestra or the athletic events (either student or
faculty team sporting events). And he always made
excuses whenever a luncheon or party was given.
"He was behind in his responsibilities," he would

always say, and it was usually true, but almost no one knew that he was responsible for his own assignments and he gave himself more to do than anyone would really be capable of doing.

He didn't dislike people. He was shy. He was perfectly capable of carrying a conversation, as long as that conversation was about technical aspects of the behavior of magic, the interaction of energy transference among the inner and outer planes, spell casting in general, or the history of The Church. These were the things he knew. These were the things he could talk about with confidence. Ask him about anything else and it was likely he would turn red and begin to stammer being unable to make polite conversation about common everyday things.

This was something new. This idea that someone had romantic, or maybe simply practical, interest in him from a relationship standing was too much for him to comprehend. He knew he was not an unattractive man. He was fit, if not strong, and his face was free from any serious defects or so he liked to believe. But no one had ever shown any interest in him in that way. He could not remember any woman ever asking him to a school dance, a walk on the beach, or an evening in the city.

Now he was beginning to wonder just what might be wrong with him, anyway, that he hadn't been approached before now by at least one woman. Was it all him? Was he so introverted that he gave out clear signals that to approach him was a waste of time.

Why would his mind even have such ridiculous questions? These were not the things of importance right now. He was missing something. He had to be. There was a connection to all of this and he was not about to let himself believe otherwise.

Hiram stayed in his apartment for the rest of the evening. When the eight o'clock services were completed he changed out of his robe and into a casual shirt, with a light vest, something long (he liked to be able to put his hands in his pockets when he was nervous so that he didn't fidget, or bite his nails). When he had finished putting on his socks and shoes, there was a single light rap at his door. He went to the door and opened it. No one was there.

On his doorstep was a small square vial. It was short and made of thick clear glass. Inside of the vial was a dark amber colored liquid. The neck of the vial was very small barely the size of a piece of straw and closed up with a cork. There was a piece of thin paper underneath the vial. He picked up the vial and the paper. The paper was a note. Written in rough script was the message, "Keep this clos, just in cas," written just like that, with simple misspellings. He was about to put the vial down on the table close to his door when the paper began to disintegrate in his hand. There was a small puff of smoke that smelled faintly of banana oil and a sizzling sound, as if the paper had been ignited, but no flames appeared and in just a couple of moments the paper was gone.

The sun had set and the moon was low in the sky, three quarters full. The campus was dark except for a few oil lamps placed along the walkways between the larger buildings, but these were hardly enough to make it possible to see every corner. Basically the lamps provided just enough light to allow people the benefit of not getting lost if they had to go out in the dark. A few clouds were in the sky making the stars almost impossible to see, and the pale light of the moon cast long blue-grey shadows across the grassy field in front of the dormitory. Tall full trees, olive, plum, and pear trees, their leaves dark masses swaying in a light breeze from the north made strange sounds in the shadows creating an eerie scene that made Hiram feel a bit apprehensive.

Hiram looked to the left and to the right for any sign of the person who placed the vial and note but could see no one. He was about to dismiss the whole affair when he noticed a dark shape in the branches of a pear tree a dozen yards from his front door.

For some reason he found his mind drifting back to a book by a reclusive hermit who wrote of the spiritual fulfillment attainable by the direct practice of divination spells cast exclusively upon the caster himself. It was a short work, written forty some years ago, and the most enduring aspect of the book was its insistent reminder of the importance of perception of one's surroundings without the expression of awareness. A notion the author referred to as still sensory engagement. It came back to Hiram, now, that he had been so fascinated by that book, when he was seventeen, that he practiced for years the techniques without being conscious of it most of the time.

With little or no conscious awareness Hiram was now practicing those methods again. He gave away no signal, no fault of body language, no turn of his head or widening of his eyes to alert the figure in the tree that he had spotted who ever it was. He made a pretense of having difficulty putting the vial into his vest pocket as he took note of the particulars of the shadowy figure. A small person dressed all in black, garments close fitting, crouched on a thin branch trying to hold the body still and stretched out in mimicry of the tree itself. About six to ten feet from the ground with the head turned sideways and the chin tucked down.

Leaving his door open Hiram walked to his desk and sorted through the letters of introduction until he found the two he needed. He gathered them and then left pausing at the door and verifying that the figure in the tree was still there. She was. Madame Dorchester's letter had said it would be a she, and that he was not to take notice of her.

Part 8

Madame Dorchester's office was across the campus
to the north toward the student housing complex. As
Hiram made his way across campus he noticed the
frequency of oil lamps increased to the point at
which each lamp post was only a few steps from the
next. It had been a while since Hiram had ever
ventured out of his apartment after evening services
and he remembered that when he was a student
there had been no lamps at all.

He suspected he was being followed by the shadow
person, but he didn't do anything to confirm his
suspicions. As it was he was keenly aware of the
sounds his own shoes made on the gravel stone
walk. It was the only sound around him and it was
an uncomfortable sound.

Hiram approached the building where Madame
Dorchester's had her office. Hers was on the third
floor of a very old building that had once been a
watch tower back in the days when the university
buildings were part of a castle compound. The
tower was a slim structure over fifty feet tall. The
top floor had been turned over to document storage
for the university's more mundane records. Many of
the non-teaching university staff had offices in this
building. It was close to the road that led away from
the school toward the Ranchello district of the city
of Las Rotavas. The Ranchello district was a stretch
of large estates close to the beach to the north.

Some of the those estates, once ranches that managed grazing cattle or goats (many years ago when Las Rotavas was a frontier town between the port city of Cabretto in Liegridan and the city of Dromallo on the other side of the rugged hills and bleak canyons of central Theeth), had been remodeled into housing complexes, apartments for wealthier students and some university staff and small hotels that catered to families vacationing on the North Shore.

When Hiram was still in the mission school, when he was in his last year there, he became obsessed with the history of Liegridan particularly the area of Cabretto. Cabretto was once a kingdom ruled by a succession of monarchs from the family of Lieger. The city of Cabretto was over six hundred years old. Hiram studied all he could about the migration of people from the east, from Anthandra, across high mountains and deserts onto the plains of Liegridan over twelve hundred years ago. Settlers moving in vast trains of wagons or even on foot (numbering, according to some sources, in the thousands) settled into fertile valleys and along the dozens of rivers and streams that ran down from the high mountains separating Liegridan and Anthandra toward the sea known as the Ses Mar. These settlers created, at first, family ruled communities that evolved their own sets of laws and customs. Until the whole of Liegridan counted not less than twenty three separate kingdoms (though many argue that most of these so called 'kingdoms' were only kingdoms in name and pageantry as toward the end of that period in history most of the smaller kingdoms were in fact loyal and subservient to one of three Great Kings of Liegridan). That was before the plague of 872 when the population of Liegridan was reduced by nearly fifty percent, over a million dead (in other parts of the continent even more). His interest in history eventually led him to study the history of The Church itself, and in this area it was said that few had learned more in as little time as he had.

There was something about Hiram's fascination with history that set him apart from most others. It was not just that he could tell you the details of any important event by date or by personages. No the art of memorization was nothing special among the students of the University. It was part of the curriculum that those who sought to take holy vows studied various disciplines of memorization for at the heart of casting divine spells was the memorization and repetition of lengthy prayers.

Hiram's interest in history was more philosophical. He had written many papers expressing his thoughts about the development of culture, and religion, based on the history of the movement of various peoples across the continent. It never ceased to fascinate him that as one people, with a fixed set of traditions and beliefs, came into contact with another people something strange would occur (often resulting in wars that attempted genocide). As the dominant culture struggled to eradicate the weaker culture they would not realize a new culture rising up from the tragedy slowing replacing everything that was cause for the conflicts in the beginning. And he had never read of a situation in which one people, believing themselves superior, made war against another and in the end managed to keep their beliefs intact. It was a great cultural mystery to Hiram and he would spend the rest of his life learning more and more about it.

Again Hiram found he was letting his mind wander. The walk to the tower took him less than a quarter of an hour and in that short time he had lost his focus on why he was even going. It was one of those moments, not unusual for him, when he found he was already ascending the stairs that wound around the outer wall of the tower and had reached the second floor landing before he remember what his purpose was. He paused for a moment, checking the letters in his hands, and noticed the shadow person had stopped below the stairs near the corner of the tower behind him. The shadow person stayed still and stood close to the stones of the corner where they bulged outward creating a dark hiding place that would have concealed her completely if it were not for a poorly placed hand against a stone whose surface was reflecting a small bit of moonlight. Again Hiram made no sign that would give away that he had noticed the shadow person but inwardly he smiled to himself at how easy it was for him to spot her.

Hiram hurried up the next flight of stairs, which turned the next corner of the building bringing him onto its southern face and at the third floor landing.

A small archway gave access to the interior of the tower from this landing. At this floor the interior was a cross of two hallways. On the ends of three of these hallways were balconies, one at the north, one at the west, and one at the east. The southern side landing was for the stairs. The quartered sections of the third floor were each one separate office and Madame Dorchester's was in the southeast corner. The door to her office was straight down the hall and just before the intersection. He slowed his pace and took a few deep breaths before arriving at the door. He didn't want to appear to be out of breath. He knocked gently, four times, and the door opened immediately.

Madame Dorchester opened the door and reached for Hiram's arm to pull him gently but quickly into the room. There were many large candles in sconces on the walls that filled the room a yellow glow. Hiram saw that the Captain and another woman he though he recognized were waiting in the room near Madame Dorchester's desk, which was placed near the wall opposite from the door. The Captain was still wearing the same uniform she had been wearing earlier in the day when she had spoken to Hiram outside of his apartment, and the other woman, a tall slender woman with long auburn colored hair, wore the deep blue robe of The Church with a white vestment over that. Around her narrow waist was a thin green cord knotted above right her hip. The white vestment marked her as a high priestess and Hiram thought he recognized her as one of the assistants to the reverend mother. She seemed very familiar. Something about her face was characteristically unique. Her face was long and her checks high. She had a small nose and exotic almond shaped eyes. She was a strikingly beautiful woman. Madame Dorchester was dressed in a heavy dark grey robe with a narrow green belt. It was unusual for her to be dressed in this way and Hiram wondered why she had chosen the more traditional garb (robe and sash) rather than her normal professional attire of a suit with a long coat.

As soon as the door was closed behind him, Madame Dorchester introduced the other woman. Holding out a hand toward her Madame Dorchester said, "Hiram I would like you to meet the High Priestess Mistress Marjory Dalinas. I'm sure you know who she is. She is here to speak for the reverend mother on behalf of The Church at Ses Theeth."

Hiram had never directly spoken to Mistress Dalinas, but he knew of her reputation. He knew that she held significant power in the university administration and was possibly the second most powerful woman on the campus.

The Captain and the High Priestess were standing on opposite sides of Madame Dorchester's desk, just a few steps away from him. On the desk between them were two odd looking bundles. The first bundle appeared to be a stack of expensive books while the second bundle looked like a set of very small leather satchels. The kind of small leather satchels that fashionable people in the city wore slung from narrow strips of leather over their shoulders or tied to a belt. He couldn't count how many of the satchels there were exactly as they seemed to be stacked and arraigned as if the group of them made, when joined, a single shoulder pack but at the same time it was altogether obvious they could be separated into individual pieces. He had not seen anything like these bundles in Madame Dorchester's office in the past weeks any time he had been here before and wondered why they were here now.

Hiram moved to stand in the center of the room and said, "I came as you told me. I don't understand what is going on."

"Let me explain a few things if I may," Marjory said as she placed her left hand on the stack of books on the desk. Her voiced was hushed, barely above a whisper. "The events transpiring in the town of Rainwash have been known to The Church for over half of a year. An exact course of action had been decided upon by The Church Council almost immediately but advice from many of the Sisterhood swayed the Council to keep that plan secret for many weeks. It is important that what I tell you next you do not let go to your head. I, as well as Madame Dorchester, the reverend mother, and the Captain, have known about you and your particularly special intellect for quite some time. You might like to know that I personally, at the request of Madame Dorchester, have written three of the letters submitted for your review before the Council. Your vast knowledge of the history not only of The Church but of the continent in general, as well as your demonstration of a comprehensive understanding of the subtle differences between the arcane and divine arts has not been taken lightly. Your achievements are known to every member of the Collective. It was decided very early on that you should be one of the individuals involved in this mission. I apologize that much of the planning for the mission The Church has selected you for has been done without your involvement, and to a great extent the involvement of your direct lead, Madame Dorchester." Here the High Priestess took her hand away from the books on the desk and walked toward Madame Dorchester. "Rubynna," she went as she placed a hand on Madame Dorchester's shoulder, "Who was once herself a Sovereign Sister in good standing, was left out of the planning for reasons that have been explained to her."

The High Priestess moved close to Hiram and motioned for the Captain to gather in closer as well. Her voice became even softer as she went on explaining things to Hiram.

"Every necessary arrangement for your participation has already been cleared by the Council and they await your arrival in Ses Theeth to brief you on your task," she said.

Hiram stepped back suddenly. Unable to raise his own voice above much of a whisper he said, "I am going to Ses Theeth?"

"Yes. You are going to Ses Theeth. Tomorrow you will request an audience with the reverend mother to request permission to go but it is all just a formality at this point. You will stay here, at the university, for ten days. That will be long enough to receive some specific training and instructions about the mission and to attend the spring festival as the Captain's escort."

At the mention of the spring festival Hiram noticed the Captain's face seemed to twitch slightly near the corners of her mouth. Hiram knew that there was more to this part of the plan than they were telling him. There was some complication with him being her escort. At the awarding of the letters it was obvious there was some confusion in that he had not already been asked to go to the festival. Hiram remembered what that the Captain had said. That she had honestly wanted him to trust her and to know that she trusted him. It seemed to him now that she had specifically avoided talking about the festival at all. Was there something about this that troubled her? Was he, after all, unappealing to her in some way? Was she being coerced into this part of the plan such that she had not been able to go through with it? And why did they need to attend the festival at all?

Part 9

"Hiram are you listening?" Marjory asked interrupting Hiram's thoughts.

"Yes I am," he answered, "But I don't understand the significance of the festival, or why I must attend."

At this point Madame Dorchester had to tell the High Priestess the unexpected news that the Captain had not already asked him to be her escort.

The High Priestess walked slowly around to stand behind the small desk, all the while looking downward as she held her right hand close to her mouth. Finally she looked at the Captain and asked, "Why did you leave that off? Was there something we needed to discuss? I thought we were all very clear on this point."

"I thought that I should take some time getting to know young master Whales and I felt that if I had an opportunity to speak to him again latter in the day I would ask him then. I had not counted on the letters being ready so quickly. I had hoped I had at least three or four hours before the presentation would be made."

Hiram knew it was a lie, because when they had parted company the Captain had not mentioned coming back to see him later, in just a few hours.

By the look on her face, Hiram suspected the High Priestess did not believe the Captain's explanation either.

"Hiram, what did you and the Captain talk about this afternoon?" Marjory asked.

Again Hiram remembered that the Captain had said she wanted to trust him and specifically asked for his trust as well. He remembered how honest and kind the Captain's mother had been and he felt that he could not now bring himself to violate that fledgling trust. He decided to bide his time, not lie to the High Priestess, but tell her what he could without exposing the Captain and then make a point of speaking to her later.

"We talked of the memories we had of her mother who was a Sister at the mission school where I was sent when I was a twelve years old. Did you know the Captain's mother Mistress Dalinas? She was very special to me, very kind, and probably the biggest reason I became so interested in reading old books."

"I only knew her casually but yes I knew her. She past away only a year after I arrived here in Los Rotavas," the High Priestess said. "I have been told she made a great impact on many people in the city. I can understand that the two of you would have this in common and how it could have distracted the Captain from the plan."

Marjory moved from behind the desk to come closer to the Captain. "The reason the Captain was to ask you to the festival was two fold Hiram, first for your protection, to create a convincing reason for the Captain to justify sending her agent with you on this mission. The second reason is a bit more complicated and is meant to be a sort of double ruse and possibly confuse those who are acting against our interests."

"Why do I need protection?" Hiram asked, "And why would our going to the festival give her reason to justify sending someone in her organization with me?"

For the first time in his dealings with the three women he sensed he had touched on something they were uncomfortable with. The three exchanged awkward glances and the High Priestess even turned away to make her hands busy with the bundles on the desk.

"You see Hiram," Madame Dorchester began to say having trouble getting the words out. "It is not going to be easily accepted that the agent of the Captain is traveling with you, particularly when it involves her sleeping in the same room as you do. That isn't generally accepted. You understand what I mean?"

Hiram was shocked into silence.

"Now try to understand," She went on. "It is important, very important, that you be protected during this mission and there is every reason to believe that your life will be in danger from agents working for the senate of Liegridan, as well as the agents of other religious organizations. And I, or Mistress Dalinas, can explain to you why that is later. So it was decided that, well, it's like this…" she couldn't seem to go on and the Captain picked up the explanation instead.

The Captain approached Hiram and put her hands on his upper arms, taking a firm but not tight grip as she looked him straight in the eye. She was slightly taller than Hiram and it made the moment even more awkward for him. "The decision was made that at the festival in the presence of many people who, most likely, report to the enemies of The Church and the Sovereign Sisterhood I would propose marriage. You were to accept the proposal, but on the condition that you be allowed to undertake a serious mission at the request of The Church. I would naturally agree but demand that to protect my future husband from any possibility of temptation you would agree to accept my agent, Sister Tiranna Garchias, as your Antodereo, the official chaperone of the courtship rituals of the noble houses of Liegridan. There would be no reason for anyone to question this request and you would be under no scrutiny from The Church. There are many within the Collective, some who have been Sisters themselves, who would not want a member of the Sovereign Sisterhood included on this mission. This plan was devised to ensure you had the necessary protection and that the Sisterhood would be involved, and I have to be honest with you, it is practically fool proof."

The Captain released her grip on Hiram's arms and backed up a step going on with her explanation. "Outside of the Council there is only mild speculation that you are to be sent on this mission. We knew that announcing it officially at the festival might actually give our enemies reason to believe you might be a decoy, and that maybe this sort of public announcement would come across as a poorly staged 'theater of the absurd'. It is possible that our enemies would waste days running around in circles trying to discover the identity of the real operative, giving you that much more of a head start."

"At this moment we already know that members of other religious followings are sending representatives to Rainwash. We have heard that the town is in some sort of state of chaos. Don't be alarmed we have good intelligence that your sister is safe. It would seem she refuses to share any information she is gathering, and we believe you might be the key to finding out what she knows. These other interests have learned not to threaten your sister. It turns out that in the last year she has improved upon her skills and knowledge of arcane wizardry and is more than a formidable opponent for any run of the mill cleric. The lands around Rainwash are still contested, and the Clan leaders of

Holdandun would not react kindly to any armed threat moving though their territories toward Rainwash. Fortunately for us this has kept any real threats out of the area. Right now our best hope of determining what is going on in Rainwash is to get you there and learn what your sister knows. We need you for many reasons. Because of your talents, because of your character, because of your relations, all of these things come together in you in very convenient ways. We are not just counting on you. We are placing all our hope in you. We need to keep you safe and keep everything you learn from your sister safe until our suspicions are confirmed."

It was too much to take in at once, and the strain was obvious on Hiram as he struggled to understand everything they were telling him. He shook his head for a moment and finally asked, "How much danger am I in now? How much worse is it going to get?"

Hearing the concern in his voice the High Priestess rushed toward him. "The real danger right now is very slight. We are only having you followed to check to see if anyone else has thought to focus on you or make inappropriate contact with you. Right now we don't think anyone wants to harm you. They might just simply want to approach you and bring you into their confidence. Possibly even offer you a considerable payment for any information you have or that you may acquire. It is a complex and delicate matter we are trying to ascertain, one with far reaching consequences. Do you understand what I am saying?"

"Yes of course," Hiram said in his automatic voice. The statement made the Captain smile. "But you didn't tell me how much more dangerous it will become," Hiram said after a short pause.

The Captain answered him before the High Priestess could. "Once they understand what we expect you to do, and they believe you will do it, and cannot be bought, they may think they have no other recourse but to kill you."

Hiram felt the blood drain out of his face, and a warm feeling rise in his neck.

The High Priestess put a hand out to lightly push the Captain aside and said, "But let me assure you. As long as you are close to the Captain's agent, she will do everything she is trained to do to prevent that, even if she must sacrifice her own life. There will be other agents of The Church, of the Sisterhood, and possibly many others we don't have complete information about yet near you, staying close but without getting to close. It might prove that in time these others will show themselves to be allies and not enemies. This thing we are dealing with could turn out to be nothing at all like what we are suspecting, or it could prove to be a threat not just to the authority of The Church but to the lives of every one on the continent."

"Can you at least," Hiram swallowed hard as he tried to speak. "Tell me what it is we are dealing with, or at least what you think we are dealing with?"

"Not at this time," Marjory announced in a regular voice.

The High Priestess stared hard at Hiram and then lowered her voice back to a whisper. "We cannot be sure we are not at this very moment being subjected to spying efforts of our enemies. The tower itself has been infused with lasting low power enchantments that prevent scrying efforts, not by blocking them as that kind of magic may attract unwanted attention, but by merely scrambling or distorting any such efforts. However, a spy may be close enough to overhear us, simply by using enhancements common to either the divine or arcane arts."

Hiram nodded his understanding.

Madame Dorchester took Hiram by the hand and said, "I think we may have overdone it just a bit for one night. But we wanted to tell you what we could now. In the next few days it may become very confusing to you and we need you to be in the best frame of mind. There will be many things we will ask you to do. We need you to be focused and sharp for the next couple of days. Once you are in Ses Theeth you will be able to relax before the mission itself begins. You will be closely watched and protected so try not to be too nervous as you go about your daily activities. For now, and until we tell you otherwise, nothing we tell you should be written down. Try and commit it to memory. You must be diligent about this. Keep your mind clear of trifling details and go along with us as easily as you can. I really believe you are the only one who can do this Hiram. Many people share that feeling. Go back to your apartment and try to get some rest as best as you can. We will stay here a few more minutes and work out a plan to get you publicly asked to be the Captain's escort. It will probably be ready to be put into action by tomorrow night. Just try to rest tonight. I will come and see you first thing in the morning." She spoke in a soft soothing tone as she walked him the few steps to the door and opened it.

"I never imagined my sister's letter would lead me into something like this," Hiram said as Madame Dorchester opened the office door.

"You must have suspected something serious was going on in Rainwash?" The High Priestess whispered.

"Well yes I suppose I should have. Some of the things she described were fantastical to say the least."

Again the women exchanged nervous glances.

"Perhaps," the Captain said, "You should turn that letter over to us for now."

"Of course," Hiram said automatically, reaching toward where his jacket pocket would be if he were still wearing his suit. Realizing he had changed clothes since then he said, "I left it in my suit I will get it and bring it right to you since you will be here a bit longer."

A slamming noise startled them all as a figure in a dark cape and leather armor suddenly jumped from somewhere above the northern balcony and landed hard on the wooden surface. It crouched for only a split moment and then leapt over the rail away from them.

From inside the office the Captain said, "That would be my agent already on her way to retrieve it. Don't worry again about it."

"That was your agent?" Hiram asked pointing toward the balcony. "I knew your agent had been following me here. The shadow person dressed all in black. But she wasn't wearing a cape."

"What!" the Captain shouted and bolted past Hiram toward the balcony. The rest of them hurried after her.

The four of them reached the balcony in time to see two figures running as fast as they could away from the tower, one figure running ahead of another, separated by only a few yards. The first figure, the one wearing the cape, was losing ground to the second, the shadow person.

Part 10

Earlier that day Tiranna Garchias was back in her apartment folding the blue clerical robe that had been lent to her by the High Priestess, and reflecting on her encounter with Hiram Whales (the man who would save the world?) when she heard the apartment door open and then the voice of the Captain.

"That went well, even if a bit awkward there at the end," the Captain said.

"The man is an idiot," Tiranna said as she placed the robe into a hidden compartment in the wall. For the last three months Sergeant Tiranna of the Order of the Crimson Blade of Saint Honoree had been impersonating a student at the university. She was renting an apartment on the prestigious Federico Boulevard north of the campus, on the beach. Tiranna had enrolled in one class taught by Hiram, and kept close to him without being noticed almost continuously. Her wardrobe consisted of numerous garments in a dozen different styles, as well as four wigs of varying cut and length. She hated the routine of having to change clothes every few hours, keeping some garments hidden in locations all across the campus, when she had already discovered that the man she was supposed to protect was so impossibly scatter brained that she believed she could walk around on campus in her dress uniform and still he would not notice her.

"That is an uncommonly harsh assessment, even for you," The Captain said. "It was probably a bad idea, on my part, to have you monitor him from a distance for so long. I think that once you get to know him your opinion will change."

"Doubtful, with all due respect Captain. In the past two months alone I have been right at the man's elbow for several minutes at a time and he never raised his nose out of the book he was reading for even a moment. I could have pinned a flower to his ear without him noticing. And this afternoon, if I had not forced him to notice the letter I honestly believe he would not have seen it for a week. No I can see it now," the young Sergeant began walking around her apartment stiffly in a poor impersonation of Hiram, her tone full of mockery, "Oh I have these letters to deliver, of course, of course. I will take one at a time from the stack and deliver them one each day. Of course, must be exact about these things, of course."

"Sergeant!" the Captain said. "That will be enough. I should not have to remind you that you have taken a vow to be committed to this mission. That it is no secret to any of us that our own sisters, dividing themselves every day over matters far more trivial, will be watching us from every chapter looking for any reason to denounce this, you, me, our orders. Your superiors made it clear to me that you were the best woman for this assignment. I have placed a great deal of my own trust, faith, and career in those recommendations. Do not presume that I will hesitate in the slightest to dismiss you if I have to and do this on my own."

"Forgive me Captain," Tiranna said. She felt the painful sting of the honesty in the Captain's words. She had been warned, by her own superiors, that her quick tongue and hot temper would be trouble for her. Her promotion to Sergeant was not even one year past and she had already been written three disciplinary remarks of judgment. One more and she risked being stripped of her rank.

"I am very sorry," she went on, getting down on her knees and folding her hands in front of the Captain. "I have no excuse for my behavior. Please forgive my impertinence, but I am having so much difficulty seeing this man for all the things you and the others see. I have been trained to react quickly to situations and sometimes I react quickly in ways I should not."

The Captain stared with cold eyes down at the small sergeant letting the young woman sit quietly with her thoughts for a long time before finally saying, "Your outbursts are your greatest fault. You speak too often without thinking. Discretion, in all things, is the best virtue for a sergeant in the Sovereign Sisterhood. I know that you are of one of the Orders more honed for action, and less for the discipline of diplomacy. Let us both hope that this 'training' you speak of is all that you believe it to be. But regardless of your own ideas about your abilities I will continue to demand that you practice as much self discipline as you are able."

The Captain went to leave Tiranna's apartment stopping at the door she said, "Hiram will be leaving his room after evening services. You are to follow him. He will meet with the High Priestess, Madame Dorchester, and I in the north tower. I expect you to have a full report of any unusual behavior from anyone who may contact or approach him. Until then I strongly recommend you keep to the prayers of discipline rather than waste your time in any of those 'training' exercises they taught you in Holdandun. I want you to be as sharp of mind as you are of body and at the moment you are demonstrating a strong imbalance of the two. There is still a very good chance that this assignment may redeem you in the eyes of your superiors, and you absolutely do not want to be reduced in any way in mine."

With that the Captain left closing the door hard behind her.

Tiranna stood up slowly, took a cleansing breath, and then let out a physical scream. Her body arched backward, growing as taunt as a stretched rope. She raised her arms above her head and opened her mouth wide. Her posture was an outburst of emotion and yet she made no sound.

Oh how she hated herself. Every time she was this close to proving she was worthy of her rank she would go and stupidly, casually even, behave in childish ways, and always right in front of a captain or a commander. Why, why, she beat at her head with her fist, was she always so irresponsible when it mattered most? Yes the Captain had told her to study her prayers, but her anger at herself was too great. She needed to unwind, and the only way to do that was through a different discipline, the discipline of the Aschinzi, the training of the silent assassins of Holdandun.

And wasn't it enough? She reminded herself. Only a handful of people, born outside of the walls of the Holdandun city of Ukarinoki had ever been allowed to train in the art of the Aschinzi. At sixteen she had rescued the Dwarven prince Teni from drowning, and proved herself worthy of their clan's highest honors when she assisted in the defense of the city from the attacks of the Gnoll War Chief Rockda. Nine Sisters gave their lives in that battle, and she, just a novice at the time, was finally indoctrinated into the Order after the graves were dug and the ashes returned to the hamth from where they came. On that day she had recited her commitment vows with four cracked ribs and still blind in her left eye. And she was only seventeen at the time, the youngest ordained Sister of the Order of the Crimson Blade of Saint Honoree in its history.

"Wasn't that enough!" Her own voice shouted in her head as she approached a wall in her apartment where two curious hooks jutted out from the wall five feet above the floor. She bent quickly at the waist and vaulted her legs toward the wall in a forward flip striking just next to the hooks with her feet as she supported herself with her hands on the floor. She smacked her heals against the wall until her shoes came off with the force of the blows and then curled her ankles into the hooks. Folding her arms across her chest and closing her eyes she began to pull her body upward, her weight hanging from the hooks, until her chin touched her knees. She let her self down slowly and then pulled herself upward again beginning the paced count to one thousand.

Tiranna had only a couple of hours until she was required to follow that man again. She could only do a third of her daily routine, but she would complete that, and as quickly as possible. She would end her exercises with a balance routine using just her right hand, and then take her time donning the sacred garments of the Aschinzi. She would do her prayers before she had her evening sleep. Tomorrow she would try even harder to prove that she was a worthy Sister, a worthy Sergeant, and she knew she could be those things and be an Aschinzi with no disgrace to either of her vows.

When she had finished, balancing on one hand while raising her legs up and down in various positions, Tiranna wiped herself down with a towel moistened with cool water and changed into the traditional garments of the Aschinzi.

It began with a body suit made from strong woven threads that was one part pants and one part chest protection. Two straps sewn onto the upper chest piece went over her shoulders and crossed behind her back, then were pulled around her waist and tied at her stomach in a flat knot that added to the protection of her mid section. A large shirt, with wrapping sleeves, was next. The shirt had no collar and the bottom was tucked up into the straps around her waist. Next came a heavy padded cloth coat, split in the back and on the sides. In the front it was wide enough to overlap itself. One flap of the coat was tied by attached short straps under the right arm, on the inside, and the other under the left arm on the outside. The coat had a stiff wide collar that was normally turned down and wore flat adding protection to the upper back, but could be flipped upward if additional neck protection was needed. The last pieces of the garment consisted of slip-on cloth shoes with stiff felt bottoms and a padded head covering that wrapped around in a complex manner leaving a very small gap where the eyes and mouth were. There was ceremony involved in the donning of the last articles and Tiranna reminder herself not to rush through it. Taking her time, and breathing in a rhythm, she finished with the traditional garments of the Aschinzi assassin with great pride.

Tiranna left her apartment not through the front door but through a small window that led into an alley from her washing room. She made her way through the growing shadows as the sun was setting being careful not to be seen by anyone. This tradition, the art of stealth and practice of body control, was the very foundation of the Aschinzi training. Weapon skills and hand to hand combat techniques were all built upon this foundation. The Aschinzi was part acrobat, part shadow, and part warrior all at the same time.

By the time she had crossed this part of the city and reached the campus the sun had set. She realized that evening services would be finishing in just moments, coinciding with the setting of the sun. She hurried, moving as quickly as she dared while always avoiding detection. She moved along the walls of various buildings in such a way that her progress toward Hiram's apartment was a zigzag of sprints and crawls that eventually brought her to the stand of trees in front of his door. She had to leap just slightly in order to reach a low branch on a tree that was well suited for disappearing into the foliage. Once in place she extended her legs, toes pressed tightly against a small branch, and positioned her head and arms to blend into the natural shape of the tree. Her hiding was, in her opinion, her best talent.

Not long after she was in position a tall woman in a dark brown cloak ran up to Hiram's door. With her head bent downward Tiranna could only make out the shape of the woman from her chest downward. Moving swiftly, the woman knelt down and placed something on the ground in front of the door and then rose, knocked (only once) on the door, then sprinted away from the building passing directly under the branch Tiranna was standing on.

"Fool," Tiranna hissed to herself. "If that idiot opens the door too quickly he will spot us both."

A tense moment passed and Tiranna (without daring to move her head lest she give herself away) lost sight of the sprinting woman. Finally she heard the latch of Hiram's door and saw light poor into the yard in front of the building.

Tiranna was only able to see Hiram's lower legs, and a small item on the ground in front of him. Hiram bent to retrieve the item. A moment passed while he seemed to just stand there doing nothing, and then a smoldering piece of parchment flittered back down to land near his foot. Hiram moved away from the door but did not close it. Then she saw his legs again, and this time he left the room, closing the door behind him and heading off toward the north tower.

Part 11

The man moved slowly, always looking around as if he wasn't sure he was going the right way, and Tiranna reminded herself not to get impatient. She noticed his fascination with the lamp poles, and at times it almost seemed as though he were daydreaming. He would walk off of the pathway for no reason at all. After a few steps off of the gravel path he would obviously realize his error, correct himself, and return to the path.

She fell back from him as he approached the north tower and waited until he had ascended a few of the stairs before sprinting to a shadowy spot near the corner of the tall stone structure. She inched along the surface of the building slowly rounding it as she kept him in sight through the openings below the stairs where the wood was not fitted quiet so tightly. When he reached the second floor Tiranna relaxed slightly knowing that her work, so far, had been done. She made a mental note to write down, as soon as she returned to her apartment, all of the details she could recall of the strange figure and the item left at Hiram's door.

As the time passed Tiranna kept an eye on the position of the moon, and the clouds, always being aware of the places where the deepest shadows could be found. She heard a door open above her, and the faint sound of voices that she thought could be Madame Dorchester, but it was not possible to be certain. She turned her head to try and focus on the origin of the sounds and realized that if she rounded the building again, to the east side, she might be in a better position to hear what was being said.

Just as she came around the northeast corner of the building there was a loud thump from above. Then suddenly a man jumped down only a few feet away from her. She heard loud footsteps above and the raised voices of the Captain and Hiram.

Tiranna sprang into action. She threw herself at the man, who was taking a moment to regain his balance as the jump from above had been far, and he seemed to stagger a bit flailing his arms when he landed. She hit him with her right shoulder squarely in his lower back and knocked him off of his feet. Tiranna carried herself through the charge and rolled to her feet away from the man and to his right. She spun around and launched into a practiced warning.

"I am a paladin of the order of the..." she was saying and abruptly stopped when she realized the man was not there. He was running at an incredible speed away from her, back toward the center of the campus.

She had no time to reexamine where she had gone wrong and took off after the man running as fast as she could.

The two of them made a hundred yards in almost no time at all without any change to their positions. Then after a dozen more strides Tiranna realized she was slowly gaining on him. He was favoring his left leg but still running with amazing strength and speed. It was obvious to her that he was suffering a minor injury, either from the fall from the balcony at the tower, or from her attack but even more clear was the fact that if he were not injured so he would have left her behind with ease. They crossed through the campus, now and then cutting across the lighted pathways. He was headed for Hiram's apartment, which became clear as well. The building was three hundred yards away when Tiranna had closed the distance between them to only three paces. Her lungs burned and her breathing was becoming harder and harder to control. When the two of them reached the building where Hiram lived, coming at it from behind and on the right, Tiranna found the opportunity she was waiting for. The man had to change directions and turned to the left to head toward the door to Hiram's apartment. In doing so he slowed briefly. Tiranna did not turn but instead jumped to her left and tackled the man around his legs, holding fast as she did to the rough fabric of his trousers. The two of them tumbled away from the building and onto the grass in front of it.

Still holding him by the legs Tiranna curled up and drove her left knee into the meat of the man's left thigh just above his knee hoping the blow would compound the minor injury he had already shown signs of.

The man grunted in pain and tried to twist out of Tiranna's grip. She exerted all of her strength and rolled the both of them until she was above him and then tilting her head upward she again tried to warn the man.

"I am a paladin of the Order of the Crimson...Airrrrrg" She screamed as the man drove a short bladed knife down onto her left shoulder.

She had to release him. She was lucky in that the knife had not pierced too deeply, striking instead the boney part of her shoulder. A few inches toward her neck and the blade might have penetrated deep into her chest. The pain was intense, but she rolled away from the man and sprung to her feet as quickly as she was able.

The man was having more trouble getting to his own feet. She could see now from the enormous distension of his upper left leg that the large bone was broken. The blow of her knee had been critical to immobilizing him. She smiled to herself in the small but significant victory.

From somewhere on his body the man had retrieved another blade. He held them out in a fighting pose Tiranna did not recognize. She wondered how he could imagine he could go on with the fight. She wanted to give him one more chance.

"I am a paladin of the Order of the Crimson Blade of Saint Honoree, and a disciple of the art of Aschinzi. I offer you the honor of noble defeat and ask you to lay aside your weapons. I do not want to have to kill you."

From behind her Tiranna could make out the sounds of feet striking the stones of the pathways. She could not turn her back on her opponent and hoped that it was the women from the tower coming toward them.

The man shifted awkwardly to his right, dragging his left leg and breathing heavily through his teeth, he seemed to shudder, perhaps from the pain, and then he came at Tiranna shouting in a foreign tongue, "Ha'thata Kilasbratta!"

The knives were raised and the man moved with a jerk that caused him to pivot to his left from the lack of support due to his broken leg. The attack would have been quick and downward, leaving her to have to guess which side he would feign toward, a common small blade combat tactic, but he was not able to follow through. Tiranna had only to move to her right driving her right hand into the soft flesh below his ribs and feeling the hard leather of his armor resist the punch that otherwise would have ruptured the man's organs. With her left hand she took his right wrist and wrenched downward while lowering her own body driving the knife toward his groin, but she had not taken into account the man's weakened stance. He feel suddenly. His left leg snapping until the bone was thrust out of the tissue above his knee, and the knife instead found its mark in the center of the man's chest sliding past the breast bone and plunging deep into his body. Instantly, as though the knife had severed the very cord of the man's life force, he slumped downward and forward falling lifeless to the ground. Blood flowed out from below him in great quantities, looking dark and black in the pale moonlight.

Part 12

Tiranna heard heavy footsteps coming in close
behind her and turned just as the Captain came to a
stop a step away from her. Further back, and
coming at a slower pace she saw the High Priestess,
Hiram, and the woman Dorchester.

The Captain paused briefly to inspect the scene and
then knelt beside the dead man, turning him over as
she spoke sharp orders to Tiranna.

"Check the area out to fifteen yards to see if he
dropped or tried to dispose of any evidence, and
then…"

"Yes, ma," Tiranna stammered. "Ma, ma'am, ma
Captain, yes right away." Her words were slurred
and she began to stagger toward the Captain.

Tiranna felt sluggish and a strange sort of
paralyzing warmth began spreading through her
body. She was unable to focus her mind or her eyes.
The scene in front of her began to rise and fall as
though the ground were being shaken like a blanket
being tossed across a bed. Her ears were ringing,
and her mouth began to go dry. She thought the
Captain had given her some kind of instruction but
she felt herself slipping away.

Hiram came up behind Tiranna just as she was
about to topple over backward. He caught her and

could see that she was bleeding from her left shoulder. The last thing Tiranna remembered was something cold being pressed against her lips, and a bitter fluid filling her mouth.

When she awoke Tiranna was lying on a low bed in a small apartment. It was dim, but there was just enough light to see who was around her. Kneeling next to her was the Captain. The High Priestess was standing behind the Captain and Madame Dorchester was doing something on the floor behind them both.

"Where am I?" Tiranna asked.

"You are in Hiram's quarters," the Captain said placing one hand on Tiranna's forehead. Her head cover had been removed, as well as her jacket and shoes. "Her temperature is normal," the Captain went on, and then looking down toward her feet she said, "Her toes are still very blue, is that normal?"

The High Priestess went to the foot of the bed and knelt down. She took one of Tiranna's feet in both of her hands and rubbed briskly saying, "Sergeant, can you feel this?"

Tiranna tried to sit up but found she did not have the strength for it. "I can, uh" she grunted. Suddenly she felt hands under her shoulders propping her up into a sitting position. Looking down at her feet she tried not to react to the strange bruise like colors that covered her toes half way up her small feet. "I can yes Ma'am, but only slightly. It's like my feet are numb, and I can feel a tingling like pins and needles when you do that."

"She needs to be taken to the hospital as soon as possible," Hiram said. His voice soft and calm and right behind Tiranna's left ear.

"Yes I agree," Madame Dorchester said. She was busy on the floor, and Tiranna had to strain to turn her head to see what it was the woman was doing. Madame Dorchester was folding a heavy bed spread around the corpse of the man Tiranna had killed. The body had been dragged into the room and Tiranna could see the trail of blood, from the corpse, as it crossed the floor of the small single room apartment and pass under the door.

"Yes as soon as we are sure she is stable. Thank Xetas you had that curative on you Hiram. The poison on the blade may have killed her otherwise," Marjory said as she stood up and moved to stand behind the Captain again.

"I still have no idea who left it on my doorstep. I imagined it was someone working with you, or the Captain," Hiram said.

Tiranna tried wiggling away from Hiram's support trying to show him that she was strong enough to sit up on her own power. The man was not getting the message, and Tiranna had to say, "I'm fine let me go."

Hiram removed his hands, and the girl almost fell sideways out of the bed and onto the Captain before he could quickly wrap his arms around her torso to steady her. Tiranna had to put her hands out to her sides and support herself as she felt light headed from the sudden motion.

"Of course you are," Hiram said.

The words pricked at Tiranna's weary conscious.

"Oh will you just stop saying that," she stammered.

The Captain chuckled and the High Priestess blushed, turning her face away from them and reaching with her hand to hold back a laugh that tried to escape her lips.

"I'm sorry what did I say?" Hiram asked.

"What happened," Madame Dorchester said as she stood up and looked over at the rest of them.

"It was nothing," the Captain said. "The sergeant is a little bit incoherent. It must be the poison."

"Ugh, poison?" Tiranna sighed.

"Yes," said Marjory. "The man you attacked was wielding a blade coated with some kind of oil. One we," she went on as she waved her hand around the room indicating the others, "Have never seen before. Madame Dorchester has carefully replaced the blade into its sheath and will take the weapon to the hospital ahead of us for examination and identification. It is most fortunate that as you were losing consciousness Hiram administered a universal antidote. It seems someone who must have had information about the assailant left the potion on his doorstep this evening."

Tiranna was growing stronger by the minute and the memory of the strange woman at the door came back to her. "I saw a woman place something by the door just before he left to meet up with the three of you. She ran off to the south and passed under me, but I did not see her face. She was human that I am sure of." She tried again to keep her balance as she raised her hands to take Hiram's hands, now clasped at her chest, and gently remove them. He did not resist, and she felt him slide away from her. "I think I can sit up on my own now. Thank you," she said.

"Not so fast," the Captain said and reached for Hiram pulling him back to where he was, pressed close against Tiranna's back. "Hiram steady her for just a while longer."

Hiram put his hands gently on Tiranna's back below her shoulders and said, "The bleeding has stopped, but this wound needs treatment, and stitching."

Tiranna turned her head to look at the wound and came nose to nose with Hiram. She looked into his eyes and swallowed hard as a feeling of embarrassment came over her. She was about to say the wound was insignificant and would heal fine on its own but couldn't. Hiram kept staring back at her and she could not make the words come, nor could she take her eyes away from his. "What arrogance the man had," she thought to herself, "As if he was trained in surgery at all."

"I suppose he is right," Tiranna said finally looking away from him and closing her eyes tight telling herself to calm down and stop worrying about the man's short comings.

"We can carry her to the hospital now if she is strong enough," Madame Dorchester said as she washed her hands in a large bowl of water that was resting on a table next to Hiram's desk.

The High Priestess went back to the foot of the bed and examined Tiranna's feet once more saying, "No I think the antidote is working better than we expected. The color is almost gone. If we wait just a few more minutes she might be able to walk, which would do much to kept down any suspicions anyone might have seeing her being carried across campus, especially at this hour." She then folded her arms and asked, "Can you tell us anything else about the person who dropped off the antidote?"

"She would not have been able to see very much from where she was," Hiram said. "And she was placed awkwardly in the tree as well. It is something that she was able to see my door at all from the way she was positioned."

Tiranna turned her head to look at Hiram again and said, "You saw me?"

"Of course, it wasn't that difficult. I spend a lot of time looking at those trees so it was only natural that I…" he stopped speaking.

Tiranna's expression could be described as a perfect combination of a snarl and absolute contempt.

"What?" Hiram said innocently.

"I think she is strong enough to go now," the Captain said, and leaned across the bed to take hold of Tiranna under one arm and help her up off of the bed.

It was then that Hiram seemed to react with a start and said to Tiranna, "You're the girl from the ceremony of the letters this afternoon."

"Girl," Tiranna hissed. "I am not a girl."

"Well you look so young. I thought you couldn't be more than fifteen or sixteen years old. And what you just did. That was amazing. How did you…?"

Tiranna interrupted him. "I am twenty one years old. For your information I have…"

And then Hiram interrupted her, "You are in my history of civilization class. I recognize you now."

Tiranna rolled her head back and made a rude noise with her lips. "Now he recognizes me. See this is what I was talking about," she said to the Captain.

"I think that is enough from the both of you," said the High Priestess as she moved to take the other side of Tiranna in support. "Let's get moving. Leave the body here I will send for it as soon as we are at the hospital. Hiram you come with us. Madame Dorchester you go ahead of us. We may be slowed a bit. I don't want to move the sergeant too roughly. Take the blade to nurse Danielle if she is on duty tonight."

With care the High Priestess and the Captain stepped over the body on the floor, lifting Tiranna as they did, and then placed her back on her feet on the other side. The two women exchanged glances and then simultaneously relaxed their support on the small sergeant. Tiranna wobbled a bit but stayed on her feet. The Captain opened the door and they all were about to file out of the room when Tiranna said, "Where are the rest of my garments?"

"I put them with my laundry there in the corner," Hiram answered pointing to a small pile of clothing in the corner near the desk.

"You what?!" Tiranna practically shrieked, turned around and tried to step toward him, but was restrained from behind by the Captain and the High Priestess. Quickly the two women again lifted her off of her feet each taking a grip under one of her arms and then pivoted the sergeant in the air and marched her out into the courtyard.

Part 13

"Things are moving too quickly, far too quickly," Captain Rower thought to herself as she helped Sergeant Garchias across the campus toward the university hospital.

Not that the Captain was any sort of stranger to plans going awry. There had been more than a few of those kinds of incidents in her fifteen years as head of The Church's office of paranormal investigations. In the beginning it had been practically commonplace and a lot of that could be blamed on the difficulty in getting the priestesses of The Church to accept a Sovereign Sister in that role. Conflicts between the two organizations led to regular miscommunications and bad intelligence often resulting in even the most simple of plans dissipating like smoke in a gust of wind.

The important thing to do now, she knew, was stay focused on the larger issues and, as she had done with the wedding plan, not let the small obstacles create impassable walls.

"How did he know it was an antidote?" Tiranna asked as the three women moved slowly across the campus. She was growing stronger but the Captain could tell she was not yet ready to walk unassisted. It was difficult for her to support the small sergeant. Captain Rower was a full head taller than Tiranna, maybe more, and trying to keep her shoulder under

Tiranna's arm, and look as though nothing too serious was going on, required her to walk with her legs bent sharply at the knee instead of bent over at the waist.

"Professor Whales did not know what the vial contained," the Captain answered, using Hiram's title in hopes of reminding the sergeant that there were still protocols that had to be followed if any of this at all was going to succeed.

The High Priestess explained the rest. "Hiram remembered that the vial had been left with a magically disappearing note that had a cryptic message warning him that something this evening would be a threat. As soon as he took the vial out of his pocket I recognized it immediately. It is a magical antidote, not a natural one, and they are available from two wizards doing just that sort of work in the city. This particular antidote is exceptionally effective, and very costly. The hospital keeps a small supply of them, but other than that I don't know anyone on the campus who would keep one around. My understanding is that they sell for over one hundred Vuerras in the open market." Marjory was finishing her explanation as the three of them reached the hospital's entry hall.

The university hospital was the newest building on the campus and was constructed in a very unique style (unlike most of the rest of the buildings, which were at one time part of the old castle complex that had originally been a frontier outpost and then had been extensively remodeled over the last three hundred years).

The three story hospital building was made of wood and stone and resembled, that is it was made to look like, a Lacradanza period family mansion. A style of extremely large home built along the west coast of northern Liegridan some sixty years ago, but modernized and made on an even grander scale. The portico of the main entrance to the hospital was twenty feet high with square wooden columns stained in natural red wood colors and surrounded at the bases with a stonework façade. It was a building with many modern amenities including windows that could be cranked open or shut using metal gears and chains. There were well pumps located inside the building (in special rooms designed for that purpose making it a place where water was readily available). Specially designed rooms specifically for the purpose of caring for the sick and injured (a thoroughly modern concept in itself) were also part of the building. There were not very many of these 'purpose' built buildings in all of Liegridan. Most hospitals were converted buildings that might have been houses, monasteries, or even old prisons.

There was a popular misconception among most of the poorer educated people of the country that because many slight injuries and minor illnesses could be cured through common divine magical spells the very idea that hospitals were even necessary was wrong headed. This was just not as true as it would seem. What most people did not understand was that unlike the arcane spells (mastered through the study of exact word combinations, hand position repetitions, and the application of material components) divine magic relied on the will of the gods.

A cleric could pray, and in most cases the prayers themselves were spoken liturgies (often these liturgies were very old and had to be spoken in strange dialects) or brief rituals and in most cases the necessary requirements for casting a particular spell would be divinely revealed to the priest. However, this was less frequently as reliable as it was believed to be. Many spells, particularly those calling for great changes in reality, were rarely granted without some equally great sacrifice. The exact nature of the sacrifice required might not be easily understood and even learning what that sacrifice should be would require preliminary divination spells as well. The whole process of casting divine magic was not as simple as people wanted to believe it was.

The staff of the university hospital served two functions, first to treat (with magic when it was available and adequate) the injured or ill, and second to do research on the available methods for treating disease and injury through non magical means. In the latter the university hospital had made great strides. Among the staff the desire to heal was always the highest quality possessed and the hospital kept an open door to any who felt this desire, whether that person was man or woman, follower of The Church or not, priestess or sister, did not matter.

In the Captain's mind there was no greater respect than that that she held for the nurses who dedicated their lives to their work in the hospital. Something about entering this building always humbled her. It reminded her that there was always hope that the divisions among her own sisters could be healed. She had wondered, often, that if a hospital could be dedicated to a single good purpose, while staffed by so many different individuals, maybe the differences among the women of The Church and of the Sisterhood weren't so impossible to overcome either, if only everyone could see they all were working toward the same goals.

As soon as the three crossed under the open entrance archway (carved along the upper face with the message TO BE HEALED in large letters above the symbols of the various Saints and Heroines of The Church) a nurse in a light blue and white dress who had been sitting on a simple wooden chair rushed toward them, producing from a fold in her lap a small bell in the shape of a sea shell. The nurse, a very young very dark skinned woman, rang the bell loudly raising a steady alarm. Before she had crossed the twenty steps from where she had been sitting to the three women four more nurses emerged from a door to the left of them. One of the nurses was pushing a wheelchair very similar to the one the mother superior used.

Another of the nurses, an older woman, whose uniform, the blue and white dress, was crossed with a bright red sash, began asking questions. "What is the patient's name, what are the complaints?" This nurse was thin and her hair was almost all grey except for the very ends, which she wore tied with a green ribbon behind her head. She seemed frail but her words were clear and her demeanor was sharp and attentive. She was fair skinned, a rare sight in this part of the world, her features were clearly those of a Goraldun, even though her speech had no foreign accent.

It was then that they all, all of the nurses, recognized that the patient was being supported by two very important women, one a high ranking member of the Sisterhood, and the other an assistant to the president of the university.

"I'm sorry your graces, there will be a better time for questions. Saransa get the young woman into room four," said the senior nurse on duty, the one with the red sash. "This is the one with the poison injury yes?" she asked, and received two nods of yes. The other nurses took Tiranna out of the two women's arms carefully and sat her down in the chair, then proceeded to wheel her away, to the right and through a swinging half-door down a long wide hall.

"Where is Madame Dorchester?" the High Priestess asked. "She delivered the knife. You obviously know about the poison."

Hiram, who had taken a moment to gather the bundles (the books and strange bag like device) that the High Priestess had carried to his room from the north tower, came in right then behind them just as the head nurse said.

"She collapsed as soon as she arrived. She was barely able to tell us…"

Hiram pushed past the Captain and said, "Is she all right?"

The head nurse showed an expression of surprise at the impertinence of the young man she didn't know and said, "Yes Madame Dorchester is fine. It seems that what ever you people had been through was a great strain on her. She is not as young as the rest of you. She is resting and we are standing by her. We are watching her very closely."

"Oh," Hiram said in surprise. "You mean Madame Dorchester, of course. What about the young woman how is she?"

"We will get her the care she needs. The poison was identified through the use of a scroll and we have the necessary remedies to treat the particular effects. This poison is an adhesive based oil distilled from the roots of the Oleander tree and the pulpy tendons taken from the lower jaw of a Carrion Horror. It is a very toxic substance. Madame Dorchester mentioned you had a universal antidote on hand. That was tremendous luck or brilliant planning on your part. This poison usually kills in less than five minutes, unless the body can fight the immediate paralyzing effects, which I hear is not common."

The High Priestess produced the small vial from a pocket in her robe and said, "Is this the style of antidote kept in the hospital?"

"No," the nurse replied taking it from her hand. "But I know this bottle. It is from Abner Kataro, the dwarven wizard in the city. He gets these bottles, with this very small neck you see here," she explained showing everyone the bottle, "From the glass makers Trosido and Son's. It is a high quality metallic infused crystal bottle almost unbreakable. We get a supply of a similar antidote from Charlotte Hernandez, the wizard who is an advisor to the mayor. That is strange," she finished with a soft hum.

"What is strange?" asked the Captain. And then called to Hiram who had wandered away from them to stand near the swinging door, "Hiram please stay close to us I'm sure they are taking care of her as well as they can. You wouldn't want to get in their way now would you?" He held the two bundles close to his chest and looked somewhat like a schoolboy trying to sneak away from a class field trip.

The head nurse went on, but dismissed the dark skinned girl with a gesture that clearly meant that she was to return to her watch sitting at the chair by the far wall.

"Yesterday a priestess came in. A woman I didn't recognize. She asked about the hospital's treatment programs saying that she was interested in applying for a position here. She asked very specific questions about what we could do for various patients and when the subject of poisoning came up she asked specifically about the antidotes we kept and how we acquired them. She seemed very intelligent and kind. As she was leaving I told her that a woman with her interests and sense of caring would have no trouble being accepted to the staff, but then she sort of just smiled in a very disturbing way and left."

"That's our mystery woman," the Captain said.

Hiram slowly inched his way back toward the Captain, all the while looking back over his shoulder toward the long hallway as he did. "How long will it be before we can see her?" he asked.

"Madame Dorchester is sleeping now. Her skin color was very ashen when she arrived. Her breathing was shallow and she was sweating profusely. We administered three remedies, one for weakness of the heart, and two for easing muscle tension, and she will be resting for a few hours. I am going to recommend an extended period of bed rest for her as conditional to her release. This isn't the first time I have seen her like this and it is time she started taking seriously the warnings we have given her."

Hiram paid close attention to the nurse's words, nodding in agreement at almost each bit of information all the while making sounds like, "Um huh, Um huh." When she finished he asked nervously, "And the other one, when can we see her?"

Part 14

"Let me just see how…" the head nurse began to say.

Marjory cut her off and took Hiram by the shoulder gently, saying slowly, "She will be better off if we let the nurses take good care of her. We will check in on her, and Madame Dorchester, in the morning. There are still very important matters that need our immediate attention."

"Are any of you injured in any way? When Madame Dorchester arrived she was having trouble speaking clearly. We got out of her that there had been a scuffle, with some injuries, and that she had an item that needed special handling and examination. Other than that she was very short of breath and I decided it would be best to treat her rather than subject her to any questioning. Is there something else we can do for you?" The head nurse said.

"Yes," replied Marjory. "Can you spare a few of your staff to come with us back to professor Whales' quarters? There is a man there who was killed in the attack. We don't know who he is or anything else about him. We would need a couple of your nurses and a gurney if that is possible."

"Yes I will come myself," she said. "Sister Gelly," she said turning to the nurse sitting on the chair by the wall. "Tell Sister Sanoss that she is to relieve you for the rest of the watch. Go to the surgery room and get the heavy gurney and follow us as quickly as you can."

"Yes Ma'am," the young woman said as she stood and placed the small bell on the chair and left the room.

"What is your name nurse?" the High Priestess asked, addressing the head nurse.

"Donna Belize, and in the hospital I am called Sister Belize, or High Sister Belize if I am the staff duty nurse in charge, which I am tonight."

"Sister Belize, really," the Captain said in surprise.

"Yes," the head nurse said. "It was decided that a more formal but non-ranking title was needed for the nurses. It is not meant to be disrespectful to your sisterhood, and it has been very good for the hospital and for the patients. It seems people are more at ease when they know we treat each other with that kind of respect. Our male nurses are called 'brothers', but so far it hasn't had the same effect."

"Doesn't that lead to your patients thinking your hospital is affiliated with the Sisterhood and not The Church?" the Captain asked.

"Now really isn't the time for that Sister Rower,"
the High Priestess said to the Captain, as she pushed
Hiram toward the entrance. "Let's get moving."

The four of them walked briskly, in silence, back
toward Hiram's apartment. In a few moments the
sound of a gurney, its wheels wobbling on the grass,
could be heard behind them.

The door to Hiram's apartment had not been locked
and the lamp was still burning inside. Light could
be seen coming from under the door. The Women,
with the Captain leading, approached the door
carefully. The Captain leaned her head against the
door and listen for any sounds coming from within.
"Marjory, your grace, if you would stand to the
right just there," she said pointing to the right of the
door. "I will open the door and we can be ready for
any surprises."

Silently, and readying her hands for any quick
spells that may be needed, the High Priestess moved
to the spot the Captain had indicated. She nodded
her readiness and then the Captain, standing back
from the door so that she could just reach the
handle, pulled the door open quickly.

Everyone was tense, but nothing happened. The
body was still lying on the floor, face up.

For the first time Hiram looked closely at the man
trying to make out his features in the lamp light. He
was very strange looking. His skin was a dark

muddy brown and he wore a cowling that was snug against his head so that you couldn't see if he had any hair. He had a long sharp nose, and his lips seemed to large for his face. He was an ugly man.

The head nurse was the first to enter the room and went straight to the body on the floor. She placed the back of her hand against the side of the man's neck and held it there briefly.

"He has expired." She announced and then noticed a brown greasy substance on her skin where she had touched him.

"What is that?" Hiram asked, when he noticed the nurse was looking at the back of her hand.

"I don't know," she replied.

"Careful," the Captain said, and lunged toward the nurse taking her wrist and then rubbing the back of the woman's hand with her sleeve. "It is possible he was covered in some sort of poison or drug."

The greasy substance wiped off easily, and the head nurse raised the Captain's sleeve close to her face.

"It looks like simple actors greasepaint. It has no particular odor. Thank you for acting so quickly Captain. I was unwise to touch him without a more careful examination."

"Hiram'" the High Priestess said. "Find something to clean his face."

The three women bent down close to the man's neck, where the makeup had rubbed off as Hiram went to his closet for the rag he kept for dusting his room.

"His skin is green," the Captain announced.

Hiram began trying to clean the man's face rubbing hard across his cheeks and forehead. "Yes look," he said.

The man had been covered all over with brown greasepaint. He was a green color not unlike grass, but paler.

"He is a Beauvingian or an elf from the south?" Hiram said.

"No he is too small to be a Beauvingian, and too tall to be a Tradian. Take off his cowling."

Hiram lifted the corpse by the shoulder and tugged down and back on the cowling.

"Look at his ears," the High Priestess said.

The dead man's ears had been butchered. The tops had been removed.

The High Priestess knelt down and slowly raised the eyelids on the corpse. His eyes were all black showing no white at all. "Here open the blanket I must check something," she said.

The Captain and the head nurse unfolded the large blanket that was across the body. And then the High Priestess lifted one of the dead man's arms and pulled at the leather gauntlet on his hand. The heavy leather glove came off easily and all of them stared at the hand.

His hands were unpainted, green, but more strangely he only had three fingers. His hand was wide, wider than a dwarf's, and the fingers long and all of nearly equal length.

"I can't believe it," the head nurse said as she stood and moved back away from the body.

"An Eysturlun? Here in Liegridan?" The Captain asked staring hard at the High Priestess. Her brow knotted in confusion.

"Very strange," the High Priestess said. "Hiram how much do you know about the country and customs of Eysturlun?"

Hiram took a few slow steps away from them, placed the bundles he was still carrying on his desk, folded his arms across his chest and then began speaking in a clear controlled manner as if her were teaching a class, "Let me see," he said. "I've read

the book '*Three years before the sun*' by Doria
Asarmee, but I've also read the critique of that
novel by Doctor Gartomi, the dwarven expert on the
cultures of Emalia. Then also I have read, in the
published diary of General Superior Alleanna
Moritez who served in the missions of the
Sovereign Sisterhood in the countries of Ibalnd,
many stories of her dealings with the people of
Eysturlun, even though she herself never traveled
there, and how much she had come to understand
about their religion and beliefs. That's all of it that I
can remember."

The High Priestess looked at the Captain, who then
looked at the head nurse, who returned the
questioning gaze back at the High Priestess.

After a long silence the Captain said, "That's
wonderful Hiram. Thank you for telling us how
much you know. Can you, maybe share some of
that knowledge with us."

"Oh, of course, of course." he said and then he went
on, "The Eysturlun people are smaller than the
average human, but larger than an Eshian, taller
than dwarves, but slighter of build. They originate
on the southern half of the large continent of
Emalia, on the western portion. They have a
fascinating written history that goes back three
thousand years, almost as long as the written history
of the Anthandruns. They are a peculiar people,
among the Panura they are…"

"Excuse me," the head nurse said. "What did you mean by the word Panura?"

"Oh, well yes, sorry. The word Panura comes to us from the Lyph languages, the fairy races from the islands of Iseamarrdhe. The Lyph language of the Sahalyphs has a word that means intelligent spirit and it is used all over the continent of Emalia, much like the word people, but meant to include all intelligent creatures that can, on some level, communicate. It is a very useful descriptor, and I was introduced to it in professor Margreel's class, *'Introduction to non human philosophy'*. I first came across the word in the textbook we used for the class and…"

"Thank you. I understand," the head nurse said.

"Ah, where was I?" Hiram asked.

"You were telling us some things about the Eysturluns," the Captain said.

"Yes well, all right. Let me see, they are known to be a very xenophobic people, and have been involved in many wars with the Beauvingians over the centuries. They control a land that covers more than the combined size of Anthandra, Liegridan, Holdandun, and Goralda, but possibly not as large as Tradis. Their government is run by a High Priest of the Cult of Ieakah, a sun god. There is so much I could tell you about that, but do you really want to hear it. I'm not sure I know what it is you are looking for."

"Just kept that thought for a moment Hiram," the High Priestess said. "Sister Belize can you please help me get the body onto the gurney outside. I need you and sister Gelly to take the body to the hospital and see what can be done to prepare the body for burial. Tell anyone who comes into contact with the body to be very careful. There's still much we need to know about him. We may need to keep the body there for a few days until the matter is brought to the attention of the mother superior and she decides how we are going to handle his remains."

In a short time the body was transferred to the gurney and the nurses were off in a rush to get back to the hospital.

The High Priestess closed the door to Hiram's apartment and then turned slowly with a grave look on her face.

"This is more serious than I thought," she said.

"I agree," said the Captain. "I was thinking that very same thing as we were going to the hospital, even before I learned the spy was Eysturlun. I have seen only two or three of their kind in this city, and never anywhere in the interior, never in Holdandun or Goralda. I was told that they can be found along the coast of Anthandra, the east coast, but I never traveled that far. We, the Sisterhood, are taught about their cult, and what they believe, but not to any great detail. What have they got to do with this matter?"

Hiram had been quiet the whole time they removed the body and while the Captain and the High Priestess had been talking with each other. He had been going over in his mind all the memories he had of the Cult of Ieakah, when it suddenly all came together. Now he knew what it was they were suspecting. Now he knew why it was they had all been acting so seriously. Now he understood why his life was in danger.

"It is the Samarsa isn't it?" he asked the High Priestess.

Part 15

For the first time in his dealings with the High Priestess Hiram sensed that he had crossed some line. Her face clinched and she said through her teeth, "There will be no more discussion of the matter."

The Captain also must have sensed something different in the High Priestesses behavior. Before, as far as Hiram could tell, the Captain had shown respect for the High Priestess, respect for her position and authority. Now there was a sense of confrontation brewing.

The Captain stepped close to Marjory, and said more to her than to Hiram, "What is a Samarsa?"

"It is getting very late and there are plans that need to be altered, and some that need to be reevaluated completely. We should be going," Marjory said, her voice wavering.

The Captain reached out and took the High Priestesses arm in a firm grip. "What is this Samarsa, and why haven't I been told about it?" she said growing angry.

"Take your hand off of me," Marjory said, and twisted out of the captain's grip. "You were not told because we had no reason to tell you. We had no idea that it was a possibility. The possibility of this being related to the occurrence of a Samarsa was considered too small to be considered in the discussions. Our path forward in this matter was decided based upon available evidence and the facts we had at the time. This," she said and pointed at the blood stain on the floor, "has changed things, but not changed them so drastically that we are going to assume that it is a Samarsa."

"Can we calm down please," Hiram said and came to stand very close to the Captain, behind her left shoulder. "For what it matters I think you both know that I have been given little of any information. I mean no disrespect, and I understand that there is a history between The Church and the Sisterhood. I also understand that I am not in a position to make demands. Perhaps the High Priestess is right. It is late and we all need to get some rest. I think we can talk about this tomorrow."

"We can talk about it NOW!" The Captain shouted as she turned to face Hiram. Her face was only inches from Hiram's, her eyes wide in anger.

Without thinking Hiram put his hands on the Captain's forearms and said, "If that is what you want, but please don't be angry. I don't think anyone is trying to keep anyone else in the dark out of malice. I trust you."

Marjory turned away and folded her arms across her chest. She sat down on Hiram's bed and sighed, "I'm sorry."

Taking Hiram's hands in her own the Captain said, "I'm sorry too. It really seems as though we all let ourselves be too casual about this matter. We let ourselves believe that we had time to plan and that we could revise our plans at our leisure every time something like this happened. Thank you Hiram," and then she hugged him close to her.

"Things have changed so much in the last twenty years," Marjory said holding her head low. "It would take weeks for a message to get across the country. Even sending a horse to Anthandra was risky, and it might be a month before we had a reply from our priestesses living in foreign lands. Now steam powered ships cross the ocean in twelve days. We have missions in Kysjta, Eysturlun, and central Emalia, even on the islands of Iseamarrdhe. The Collective calls for us to isolate ourselves from the rest of the world and stay out of politics, while the Council and the Sisterhood expand our work as missionaries of charity. The Collective votes with their eyes looking back at a world of the past, and we," she said standing and coming closer to Hiram and the Captain, "We are the people trying to pull The Church into the world of today." She smiled but then the smile faded from her lips and her eyes began to water, "And for what? It would seem that nothing changes. In only a matter of minutes the trust we have tried to build is threatened."

"I will go now," the Captain said. "Your grace, please accept my apology for losing my temper, but before I go could you please tell me what a Samarsa is. I feel that I will sleep better tonight, and be better prepared for tomorrow, if I understand what this thing is. I suppose I feel in much the same way Hiram must be feeling. In that I owe you an apology as well Hiram. Maybe it was wrong of us to think we could bring you into this in any way other than being completely open from the beginning. If the times keep changing and we close our minds to those changes we have no one but ourselves to blame when we are left behind. I will try to treat you more like an equal Hiram, and less like just a man."

"Thank you Captain Rower," Hiram said.

"I want you to try calling me Salindis, or even Cindy, my family used to call me that when I was very young. I think that if we are going to be working, working together to understand this thing that is happening, you should call me Cindy."

"And call me Marjory," the High Priestess said. "Among those of the higher orders we rarely call each other by our titles, and as long as I am not eligible for the Collective, as long as I have no children of my own, I don't see why you shouldn't address me in the same manner."

Hiram's mouth dropped open and he managed to stammer out, "Oh I don't think I should do that."

Marjory and the Captain exchanged glances and then shared a nervous laugh, "Maybe you are right

Hiram," the High Priestess said. "I guess I just got caught up in the moment."

"This Samarsa," the Captain said, "Is it something that is too complicated to explain in a few words? If it is I understand the need for us to end this tonight and I will bring it up again tomorrow."

"The Samarsa is not a thing, it is a person, or I guess to use Hiram's word, a Panura," Marjory said.

"No. That's not true," Hiram said. "It isn't."

"What?" Marjory asked.

"The Samarsa appears as a Panura and there are no documented or authenticated occurrences of a Samarsa event other than in the appearance of an intelligent humanoid, but the Samarsa is not a living creature exactly. It is a manifestation, on the material plane, our world, of the power of a divine entity residing on another plane."

"Are you talking about the channeling of divine energy? Are you saying the Samarsa is some sort of cognizant spell? A spell that is aware of itself as a thing other than its effects?" Marjory asked.

"No I'm saying it is even more than that. The Samarsa effect is the coalescing and concentration of the most powerful energies, forces you might say, that dominate another plane of existence. It may be a heavenly plane or a lower plane, it may even be an elemental plane, and it can be extrapolated that a Samarsa could even be connected to the positive material or negative material planes, though there is no historical evidence of that sort of Samarsa event. No agreed single theory has been put forward to explain the cause of a Samarsa event, but a great deal has been written about the behavior of a Samarsa event. I believe there have even been planar excursions, some that proved fatal to the researchers, in efforts to discover the origins and causes of a Samarsa event."

"This sounds all very complicated and I'm not sure I understand it all," said the Captain. "How does this involve The Church?"

"Can I explain?" Hiram asked the High Priestess.

"Yes," she replied, "But Hiram try to be brief. It is getting late."

"Captain, I mean Cindy, in some cultures, throughout the history of Emalia, a Samarsa is worshiped as a living deity. These sorts of Cults are difficult to explain, as there is a pattern of treatment of the Samarsa, very bizarre treatment that is difficult to explain. The only cult that survives in any great numbers to this day is the Cult of Ieakah, who worship the Ieakah Samarsa whenever one is manifested, but who then, and I know this will sound ghastly, sacrifice the Samarsa before it can celebrate what would be a twenty first birthday, or twenty one years of existence, as no actual birth of a Samarsa has been witnessed. I think that what The Church suspects is that this event in Rainwash involves a Samarsa of some kind as they tend to manifest random spell like effects in much the way my sister's letter explained, and that if this were an Ieakah Samarsa the followers of the Cult of Ieakah would want to take this thing back to Eysturlun. Historically when there is an Ieakah Samarsa the country of Eysturlun becomes fanatical and tries to spread its dominance beyond its borders, there are terrible wars in the name of the Ieakah Samarsa."

"That doesn't seem like it should be so serious an issue. I was more concerned that we were dealing with a cleric casting spells outside the authority of The Church. It would be a simple matter of an arrest, with what we anticipated would be some resistance, and a trial. Who would care if these Eysturluns wanted to drag this Samarsa back to their country or not?"

Hiram looked nervously at the High Priestess, wondering if it were safe to go on in his explanation.

"Go on Hiram," Marjory said. "I think I know what you are thinking."

"What if it is some other Samarsa? What if, say, it was the Xetas Samarsa?" Hiram said.
The Captain took a step away from Hiram, shaking her head violently, causing her white hair to flash

across her dark skin. "There can't be a Xetas Samarsa, Xetas is God, and I cannot hear this blasphemy."

"I am sorry Captain, my sister. Please," the High Priestess said. "But Hiram is correct, and I know this is something you have heard before, and I know how the Sisterhood takes these matters, but even we of the priesthood have had to come to terms with this in our history. If it is going to offend you so much, then I can ask for another in your organization for help in this matter. But it is the truth. Xetas is God, God of the worlds waters, God of the life brought forth in the waters, but also not more of a God than Ieakah, who is God of the elemental plane of fire, or Uhra Goddess of the soil, and Rahavaz Goddess of the air. The elemental Gods have equal divine power and equal divine authority. It is not unique that The Church at Ses Theeth worships the divine that is Xetas, and we have had to come to peace knowing that the Cult of Ieakah is far larger than we are. Followers of Rahavaz are mysterious and secret, and no organized following is known, and the followers of Uhra fall into the druidic cults, and have demonstrated no will to organize outside of the small circles of their local responsibilities. We are learning that across the world there are other religious followings, in Emalia the Beauvingians worship old Gods, Hamth, who they see as the world itself, a primordial Goddess that is connected to the prime material plane, and this plane, and Churl, who they envision is the manifestation of the divine aspect of the Astral plane. And there are so many more. Some very powerful divine beings, and then there are those that are not real at all. Our faith is not the only faith in this world, and it is not the only authority."

All the while that the High Priestess was talking the Captain kept shaking her head and saying softly, "I cannot hear this."

"I will not hear this!" the Captain finally shouted.

"Damn it sister!" the High Priestess said back at her. Her right hand grabbed the green rope around her own waist and she exclaimed, "I still wear the colors out of respect. We went together to the Three Rivers. We served together you and I, and we saw the elven druids work their spells. I know what your vows mean to you. I took those very same vows and now I am a priestess of The Church do you not know how hard this is for me!"

The Captain began to cry and she began to shake as she came closer to the High Priestess saying though her tears, "Everything we fought for, everything we fight for now, and everything we believe you would throw away and reduce God to nothing. We dedicate our lives and give everything of ourselves because we believe we are right. We believe that God is Xetas and Xetas is God and no thing is greater than that."
Marjory suddenly threw her arms around the Captain and said into her ear, "My sister, my sister,

I will never not believe this. Nothing, no thing is greater than the commitment I have to Xetas, to my God, and to my sisters and brothers of this world. I love you my sister, and I will never reduce my love for God, but that does not mean I am incapable of allowing another to love their God with all of their being in the way only they understand. I will fight for the rest of my life those that would worship at the alters of Gods that teach that one people may make slaves of another, that life is not to be valued, that disrespect for a mother and her children should be tolerated, but I must come to understand that those who worship all that is good, all that I myself worship must be allowed to do so in their own way."

"But, but," the Captain tried to say, "Our vows, the Sovereign Sisterhood exists to defend the authority of The Church, the authority of the Ghedda to lead The Church. How can we survive if The Church itself is going to take a position that anyone can worship God, or, or Gods in any way they choose?"

It was painful for Hiram to watch the two women share so openly of themselves in front of him. He felt like an intruder, and at the same time he felt that he was now closer to them than he should be. A great trust was being place in him and he wasn't sure he understood why he was deserving of it.

"That," Marjory said pushing the Captain away and holding her at arms length, "Is why we need to send Hiram. That is why we need to send you, and I understand that in sending the sergeant we are sending you in spirit if not in body. Because what ever this thing in Rainwash is, if it is a Samarsa, and if it is the Xetas Samarsa, we need the most capable thinkers, and the strongest people of faith to face it head on and what ever happens we need to know that we all must face it together. The future of our faith depends on it, and if it truly is a Samarsa, the future of the world may depend on it."

"The world?" the Captain asked.

Hiram said, "According to the writings of the Emalians, the Beauvingians, the Eysturluns and others, when a Samarsa has remained unchecked on this plane for twenty one years the divine energy within it, the same divine energy that we channel in our spells, is set free flowing from the Samarsa in almost unlimited quantities. In the past this has caused wide spread chaos, destruction, and in some cases, though only in very old writings, the death of whole populations."

The women looked at him for a long moment and Hiram saw something in their eyes that filled him with hope. Something in their eyes gave Hiram the idea that he was equal to them in this moment.

Him? Hiram? An unlettered graduate, an inexperienced priest, a boy who became a cleric almost by accident, a man, a young man even, equal to these women. He struggled with the idea and questioned if he was even right to consider such a thing.

Part 16

"I can always count on you to remind me of what is truly important," the Captain said to Marjory. "In the beginning when I was first told about this mission I told myself not to worry. That was not what I should have done. I should have worried openly. I wish you had just told me all of your concerns from the beginning, but I respect the decision you made not to. In the future I will hold nothing back. Everything I know you will know, as quickly as I can get the information to you. All I ask is that you treat us with the same respect. We can get through this, even if it is the worst thing we can imagine."

"Captain, your Holiness, Madams," Hiram addressed them both with exhaustion in his voice. "It is very late. What do you need me to do tomorrow?"

"Yes it is late, but things must be taken care of," the Captain said. She removed her hat and took Hiram's hand saying, "Mister Whales will you do me the honor of escorting me to the spring festival?"

Without having to think about the necessary protocols Hiram answered, "With the permission of the President of the University, the honor and privilege will be mine Sister Rower, Cindy."

"On behalf of the mother superior, and with our blessing, permission is granted to you Hiram Whales. May your company be a blessing on your guest, and reflect well on the reputation of the university," Marjory added.

The three of them stood silently for a moment and then Hiram let out a nervous laugh saying, "That wasn't so bad."

The women left his room very soon after that giving him instructions to follow over the next few days. He would have meetings with the reverend mother, as well as with certain women of the campus who would ensure he was properly trained and supplied with the necessary attire to attend the festival as the Captain's escort.

He was told specifically not to visit the sergeant, and was reassured that a message of good will, and gratitude, from him would be delivered in the early afternoon. He was told that he should go about his usual business including the delivery of letters of introduction as soon as he felt he was ready to do so.

That night Hiram slept deeply but woke feeling ill. He readied himself, as he did every morning, for the classes he had to teach, there were two. And just as he was about to leave his apartment he noticed the bundles, the books and strange pack, were still sitting on his desk. He decided he had time and so off to the administration building he headed, taking the bundles with him, and asked to see the High Priestess.

Hiram was hurried into a small office and given a letter from the High Priestess that had several short paragraphs of further instructions. The letter ended without mentioning the bundles. The clerk, the one who had been instructed to give the letter to Hiram if he came to the office, was a young student, a man just a few years younger than Hiram. He was short and pudgy, and often seemed to be too stressed to think of doing anything other than exactly what he was told. His name was Jatherty Dosuellos

"The High Priestess is unavailable at the moment and she asks that you read this letter and then I am to return it to her office," Jatherty said.

"I must ask her some questions about these packages," Hiram said.

"My instructions were," Jatherty said becoming distraught, "To have you read this letter and then return it to her office. I can't help you with anything else."

"Can you at least let her know that I have these and that…" Hiram tried to say.

"I was only told to make you read the letter Mister Whales, I can't," the clerk said shaking his head and then he began to repeat the same thing.

"Of course, I understand," Hiram said giving up. He sat down on a small chair in the office and read the letter.

The letter told him that for the next week he should not be bothered by anyone he may be followed by, and that anyone with orders to protect him would be clearly dressed in the uniform of the Sovereign Sisterhood, no mistakes. Anyone else acting suspicious around him would be taken into custody for questioning. It mentioned the people he should contact, and in the order that they should be contacted. The list was long and he did his best to memorize the names and times of day. It concluded with a blessing for Hiram, and a special message that he understood very well. The special message was simply,

"With our trust, Sisters of the University"

The rest of the day Hiram walked as if he were elevated above the ground. He was filled with a sense of pride and a promise to himself to rise to any occasion and conduct himself in ways that would make them, all of them, proud of him.

He kept every appointment that had been detailed for him. He met with women who took his measurements for a new suit. The Captain it seemed had wanted him dressed in traditional noble attire, and no expense was spared in preparing the clothing. He met with women who taught him how to walk, and how to greet people as he would have to do when walking at the Captain's side. There were so many things he needed to learn and he did his best to learn everything he was taught.

Everyday he moved across the campus in a hurry, going from classes to appointments continually. All the while he tried not to notice the two and sometimes three uniformed soldiers staying never more than a dozen yards from him. People on campus whispered rumors, he knew, and he avoided any situation when someone was desperate to share with him the latest gossip. He never saw the young sergeant, and though he was worried about her, he remembered the trust placed in him, and stayed away from the hospital.

It was his greatest regret. On the fourth day, as he was leaving a long lesson in table manners with Sister Laura, a student approached him. It was a girl from his class on catalogs and records organization. Her name was Helen Lasseir, and she was from Goralda. She was a common looking young girl of eighteen or nineteen, with caramel colored skin and freckles, green eyes and brown hair that had red highlights. She had that look on her face. It was a look of shock and wonder, a look Hiram had begun to recognize. It was a look of someone who had heard something incredible and was looking for confirmation of the rumor, and most likely more details to pass on to someone else.

"Professor Whales," the girl called to him excitedly. "Professor Whales I have to tell you something."

Something was different about the tone of the girl's voice, something that sent a chill down Hiram's spine. He stopped walking away from the girl and let her catch up to him.

"Did you hear?" she said, and Hiram groaned at his own foolishness.

"I really don't have time for gossip, Miss Lasseir," Hiram said trying to once again distance himself from her.

She grabbed him by the arm and said in a sad voice, "Madame Dorchester has died."

Hiram froze where he was standing.

"What are you telling me?" he said through dry lips.

"Madame Dorchester," the girl said again. "I just heard from Professor Surray that Madame Dorchester died in her sleep late last night or early this morning. Everyone is going to the hospital to pay her last respects. Mostly everyone is saying it was her heart. I didn't see you outside of the hospital so I went looking for you to tell you in case you hadn't heard."

Hiram had to put his hand against his forehead. He couldn't understand how he had let himself forget that Madame Dorchester had also been in the hospital. He had gotten so caught up in the training schedule, and the warning from the High Priestess not to visit the sergeant, he had never bothered to check on the woman who he had cared about probably more than any other person in his life.

Now she was dead. Anger swelled up inside of him and he pushed away at the young girl in front of him, shaking his head in frustration.

The three soldiers of the Sovereign Sisterhood went into action. They raced at the girl, their batons drawn, and two of them took her to the ground roughly, while the third, a heavy set young woman with a wide face and a flat nose, took Hiram by the arm and moved him away from the scuffle.

"Mister Whales are you hurt?" the soldier said putting her body between the girl on the ground and him.

Fortunately for the girl she was knowledgeable about the practices of the Sisterhood. She did not resist, or call out, but let herself be pinned at the ground by one soldier, while the other quickly searched her for weapons, or devices.

Hiram's guilt turned to outrage. "Stop it! Stop it!" he called out. "I'm fine. She was only telling me about Madame Dorchester."

The woman next to Hiram restrained him and slowly the other two let the girl up from the ground. The girl, shaken by the ordeal, but unhurt, left without saying another word.

"Are you sure you are alright Mister Whales?" the women of the sisterhood asked him.

"Yes," Hiram replied. "I need to get over to the hospital."

He ran all the way across the campus to arrive at the hospital just as a crowd of people was being turned away by a group of nurses who had come out onto the grassy lawn in front of the entrance archway.

"I'm sorry young man," one of the nurses said as Hiram pushed through the people who were going away from the entrance. "Only hospital staff members are allowed in at this time."

"I have to get in," he complained.

"I can take you around to the rear entrance," a familiar voice behind him said. It was Tiranna.

He turned to see her standing there in her uniform, a scarlet jacket with red belt and black trousers. Her hair was pined back, as it was when he saw her days before at the letter ceremony. She spoke to the nurse.

"I will take professor Whales to see Madame Dorchester. If there are any problems you can address them to the Captain of Saint Bridgid's Order of Las Rotavas. I am under her direct orders to see to it that professor Whales is allowed to pay his respects to his superior."

"Oh you are Hiram Whales," the nurse said. "Yes you can just go in at the rear. We are keeping the entrance clear for now."

The next several hours were something of a blur for Hiram.

When he was walking toward the door to his apartment everything in his mind felt like a distant dream. Madame Dorchester had looked peaceful, and there were people around her. He could not recall any of them. He had been crying, and there was someone telling him that services were being arranged and that he would be told all of the details as soon as they were scheduled. He couldn't remember exactly how long he stood there looking at her and wondering if she could forgive him for having a hand in her death. He was filled with guilt and remorse. Tiranna didn't say a word but stayed close to him, close enough that he remembered at times she put her hand on his back.

At his apartment he stopped by the door. He stood there in silence for a long time.

Tiranna, who had come with him, said, "You should just go in and lie down for a while. I will report to the Captain. The others will stay and watch you. If you need to go out just be careful and pay attention to where you are going. I'm sorry for your loss. I didn't really know her, but I know she was loved, and respected."

"Can you just stay with me for a little while longer," Hiram said. He couldn't turn his head to look at the sergeant, but he felt so alone he couldn't stop himself from asking.

"No," Tiranna replied. "I can't do that. It would be inappropriate. I will tell the Captain how you are feeling and if she can get away from her duties she will come to see you right away. I know it. Now just go in and lie down."

Hiram opened his door, and then turned to face Tiranna saying, "That thing you did the other night. That was amazing. I've never seen anyone act so bravely. As long as you are around I don't think I will ever be afraid."

He walked into his room and closed the door behind him.

Part 17

One week before the spring festival there was a
memorial service for Madame Dorchester.

It was a small service only her family and a few
from the university were there. Hiram had never
known that Madame Dorchester had two grown
children, and five grandchildren. She had once told
him that her husband had died before Hiram ever
came to the city. Hiram stayed at the back of the
chapel, the Western Lighthouse Chapel on the
beach near the edge of the city, and watched as her
family, a sister, he also never knew she had, and the
children (a man and a woman each with their
children) passed by the coffin and placed small
pieces of paper with wishes for her safe transition to
the after life written on them onto the top of the
plain wooden box that was her coffin. Those in
attendance listened to a reading of a few sort
prayers and then they were directed outside to stand
by a railing and watch as the coffin was placed on a
small boat. The small boat was pulled by a larger
boat out into the harbor until it could almost not
been seen and then it was set on fire. The larger
boat would stay close by the burning boat making
sure the funeral was finished in accordance with the
rights of The Church, but family and friends left
quietly, knowing it would be an hour or so before it
was all over.

Hiram didn't leave his apartment for a whole day after the funeral. The rest of the week was spent trying to act as if everything were as normal as it should be. The day of the festival came, and he knew he had a responsibility to fulfill. He washed and dressed in the afternoon in the new dark black suit made just for him for this occasion. The shirt, delivered only the day before was the whitest shirt he had ever seen and the material was soft and so smooth he had never felt anything like it. When he tried it on it clung to his skin in ways he didn't like. He had to take it off, the dress shirt, and then put on a cotton under shirt, underneath the dress shirt, just to feel comfortable.

At just a few minutes passed the evening bells, the first bells that called people to evening services on the campus, a knock came at his door.

He opened the door to see Tiranna standing at attention in a dress uniform, polished boots, epaulettes of silver on the blood red jacket, and black trim along the collar. Her hair was washed, and brushed out, not pinned. She had bangs that came to just above her eyes. She wore white gloves on her small hands, and at her side was a short curved sword in a silver capped black leather scabbard.

"My lady Sister Salindis Rower of the Sisters of Saint Bridgid has arrived and requests you be escorted to her carriage waiting at the Arch of Lunniea," Tiranna said.

"Thank your sergeant I am ready please lead the way," Hiram said.

Tiranna snapped one toe to the ground behind her and spun around with precision. She walked a few steps away from Hiram's door and then executed a smart left turn. She marched in long strides toward the east end of the building and Hiram hurried to keep up with her, staying behind and just to her right.

Hiram looked around as they walked and said, "Are the other soldiers here tonight as well?"

Tiranna did not answer.

Hiram assumed she did not hear him.

"I said are the other," he tried again louder.

"No," Tiranna said from the side of her mouth. "And you aren't supposed to talk to me right now."

"Of course, right I remember," Hiram whispered.

Tiranna rolled her eyes.

It was a long walk. The Lunniea Archway, a memorial dedicated to the first president of the university, was in the very northeast corner of the university grounds, across a large grassy park used by the students for athletic games and events. The Arch, a tall stone monument, was close to the roadway that ran along the northern edge of the campus.

As they approached the Arch Hiram could see a large four wheeled carriage, drawn by two small brown horses, waiting. The carriage was open at the front end but toward the back it had a roof, with sides that had small half doors. Curtains hung down from the roof to just above the small doors, and Hiram could not see anyone in the carriage at all.

Tiranna stopped just a few steps away from the carriage, spun around again and announced, "My lady, may I present Professor, Mister Hiram Whales."

Hiram watched as the carriage rocked, just slightly, as someone in the back was obviously standing up. The small door in front of him opened. The curtain was pushed aside by a yellow gloved hand and the Captain, having to stoop slightly under the short carriage roof, stepped out onto the street.

She was dressed in a yellow ball gown that was off of her shoulders, a black corset, and white frock. The gown was fit perfectly to her. Her hair was combed straight with the sides pulled pack into a black leather barrette that was almost as wide as the back of her head. She was radiant. Hiram couldn't believe that she could look so beautiful. She walked, taking slow small steps, toward Hiram and said, "I'm happy to see you Hiram."

As she came to stand right in front of him he
noticed she was a few inches taller than he
remembered.

"You seem taller," he said nervously.

"It's the shoes," she said. She pulled up the large
skirt to show Hiram a pair of black leather sandal
like shoes with tall heels. "They are all the rage
these days among the wives of the Senators. They
are imported from Holdandun."

"My," he said exhaling as he saw the Captain's firm
strong legs, "They are something."

The Captain smiled, and then looked across the top
of Hiram's head. She frowned. "It's a good thing I
brought other shoes. This will never do. We will
never be able dance like this," she said holding her
hand up to her chin indicating where Hiram's head
stopped. "I can change in the carriage. Shall we
go?"

"You look so beautiful Salindis, I mean Cindy.
Really very beautiful," Hiram said trying to stop his
thumping heart with deep breaths.

"Thank you Hiram. Just remember what we
practiced. Do you want to go over it again as we
drive to the party?"

Tiranna had climbed into the small driving seat at
the front of the carriage. The Captain held the door
of the carriage for Hiram and waited for him.

"No," he said as he climbed into the back seat.

The Captain smiled and pointed to the front seat,
"You sit there until after the proposal, remember."

Hiram moved quickly across the short distance and
sat at the front of the carriage on a small padded
bench that faced the rear. His back was touching
Tiranna's. A small lump in his throat began to
quiver and he said quietly, "Of course, we can go
over it again if you think we should."

The ride to Senator Raimond's Estate was longer
than Hiram expected it to be. The carriage wound
through the neighborhoods just north of the campus,
then turned to the east, away from the hotels and
apartment buildings close to the beach. The
buildings of the city gave way to more open areas,
and a large estate appeared in view ahead of them.
The sun had set over the mountains to the west, and
the sky was streaked with gold, orange, and purple.
Huge flags of every color flapped in a light breeze,
coming in off of the beach, placed along the road as
it curved toward the buildings of the estate. Just
ahead of them there was a short iron gate attached
to two red brick pillars. The gate was opened. Just
beyond the gate a very large open sided white tent
was erected in the courtyard of the estate. Hundreds
of people in formal attire were standing under the

tent, holding large wine glasses, or small plates. A tall pole, higher than the tent, was set in the ground just on a grassy hill to the north of the tent, on a bluff that hung out over the beach below. Shiny ribbons in bright silver and gold hung from the top of the pole and stirred in the light wind.

The carriage came to a stop on a gravel road a hundred yards from the tent. Hiram let the Captain exit first and then he joined her. Tiranna drove the carriage in a tight circle and then back down the road toward the gate.

"Will the sergeant be joining us Captain?" Hiram asked.

The Captain moved in close to Hiram and took his hands in hers. "Hiram," she said in a flat voice, "Hiram, look at me. Look me in the eye. Now I would be a fool if I did not know you had feelings for sergeant Tiranna, and I have no objections. You are a dear and wonderful young man, handsome and capable. She is a very lucky woman to have someone like you fall for her. What ever she decides to do about that is her business, but Hiram," she leaned in close to whisper into Hiram's ear, "We want everyone here tonight to believe that you want to be my husband. It is important that to everyone here tonight you act as if you are in love, or at the least enamored, with me." She leaned away from him and said with a smile, "We can do this tonight, am I right?"

Hiram smiled at the Captain and said, "Yes we can Cindy, Darling."

"Darling," the Captain said as she turned to walk toward the party. "I like that."

The Captain led Hiram into the crowd of people under the large tent. Everywhere Hiram recognized the uniforms and attire of various important people of the city of Los Rotavas. There were senators, and officers of the Liegridan military, powerful merchants, and prominent artists. They stopped, every now and then, and each time someone would ask the Captain to introduce her companion for the evening. Hiram was amazed at the natural way the Captain would say, "He is a dear man, very special to me," or "This is our first time out in public, he is very shy," or, "We have a special relationship."

Very few people spoke to him, directly.

A waiter passed by with a tray of tall wine glasses, half full with a light red wine imported from the southern coast of Tradis. The Captain took two glasses and handed one to Hiram. She put the glass to her lips but before taking a sip she said softly, "You are doing so well Hiram."

Copying her movements, and placing the glass in front of his own lips Hiram said, "Thank you, my Captain."

The evening was growing darker and one by one a few fire pits were lit around the large tent. A small group of musicians, a quartet, sat down at the north end of the tent and began playing lively melodies written for spring dances. The music was light and slow in tempo. Many of the quests wore very stylish dresses or suits that were not particularly fitted for quick dancing.

Hiram and the Captain danced for a while, a few songs. She held him close to her, and he could not remember a time when he felt so awkward and so good at the same time.

From the main building of the estate came a flood of young children. The children of the quests naturally, who were up until now most likely being entertained in the house by clowns or magicians Hiram thought. This would give the adults time to meet and great old friends and acquaintances. The children went right to the tall pole and each took a long ribbon. The quartet began playing the traditional Ayahinndra, the merry pole dance music played each year at these parties (as Hiram had learned in the previous days).

The children danced in quick circles around the pole, weaving and twisting the ribbons as they did, while the adults gathered round clapping and chanting songs from their own childhood. This celebration went on for half of an hour and finally ended as the children were so close to the pole they could not move around it any more. A white haired man, a tall man with a large barrel chest and wearing a black uniform that had ribbons hanging from the right shoulder, was standing next to Hiram, who had at the time his arm wrapped around the Captain's. The white haired man leaned over to Hiram and said, "I much prefer the very long ago days when all of the married men would stand the pole and place it in the ground before the children danced."

The Captain leaned across in front of Hiram and said rather loudly, "Why yes General Martinez, I fondly remember those times myself. It really wasn't so long ago you know."

Hiram gave a strange quizzically look to the Captain who said as she leaned back into place, "General Martinez is very hard of hearing."

"Tell me young man," Martinez said. "How on Hamth did you get this lovely young soldier to settle down?" The general moved to stand between Hiram and the Captain, and took the liberty of kissing each of the Captain's cheeks as he finished.

"I don't know what you meant," Hiram said loudly.

"Oh," General Martinez said with a start, "Have I spoiled the surprise. Sister of the Saint of Fire, little Salindis Rower have you not told this fine young man what everyone in the city has been saying behind your back right in front of you."

"I had hoped it would be a surprise, General, but since you have tipped my hat, so to speak, I shall take the opportunity as it has presented itself," the Captain said.

"May I have everyone's attention," she went on. The children who had been playing racing games around the pole after they had finished the pole dance, came running over to see what was making the adults stand suddenly quiet.

"Gentlewomen, and my friends, senators, and guests," the Captain said her face beaming a wide and lovely smile. "I would like to take this time, and in front of all of the people I know and love, to ask this man, Hiram Whales, to be my husband."

She moved in close to Hiram. The crowd applauded and then went very quiet as it was obvious they had reacted prematurely.

"Hiram whales," the Captain said softly. "Will you marry me?"

"Yes Salindis Rower, I will. I accept," Hiram said, and the crowd began cheering and applauding again.

"Salindis, darling," Hiram tried to say over the noise.

The Captain didn't hear him. This was the part where he was supposed to tell her about his mission, but instead the crowd grew louder and louder and Hiram realized that among the cheers of congratulations, there were calls of, "A kiss, a kiss!"

The Captain leaned in close to Hiram and said, "I hadn't thought of this."

Hiram whispered back to her as she suddenly hugged him close to her, "I am supposed to tell you about the mission now."

Squeezing him tightly against her chest the Captain placed two quick kisses on his cheek and whispered, "We'll get to that just play along for a moment."

The crowd groaned as some people shouted, "That's no kiss. Give him a proper kiss, a proper kiss."

Suddenly the Captain took Hiram's head in her hands and laid a kiss into his mouth that stunned the crowd into silence.

Hiram felt his legs might fall out from under him.

The Captain's kiss was passionate, full of fire, warm and tender. He kissed her back closing his eyes. He had never been kissed before.

When she pulled away Hiram had to keep himself from chasing after her lips.

She stood looking at him and Hiram could not imagine what was going through her head. She was smiling, but her eyes seemed lost and distant. After a brief pause and two or three blinks of her eyelids the Captain said, "Just like the first time, darling."

Part 18

For the next few minutes Hiram and the Captain
were approached by nearly everyone in the crowd to
shake hands, give hugs, and offer warm
congratulations. It looked to Hiram as though he
would not be able to make his announcement about
the coming mission. It was the Captain who gave
him the opening he needed, when she was asked by
a curious guest exactly when the wedding would be.

"I hope it will be soon, but I don't want to keep
Hiram from pursuing his doctoral degree, which he
only told me this week he had been granted
permission to begin working on. Outside of that I
can think of nothing that should be standing in our
way," she said taking Hiram's hand. "Can you,
darling?"

"Well yes there is one small thing," Hiram said and
then went into the speech he had practiced. "I have
been asked to undertake a mission for the benefit of
the university at the request of The Church at Ses
Theeth. I am to travel to Ses Theeth in a few days
where I will learn the details of the mission. I don't
expect it to be something that will keep me away
from you for more than a few months, but I hope
you can be patient with me until I know more
details," he finished in one breath, and then after a
gulp of air added, "My darling."

A series of hushed whispers sprang up around them, people in the crowd speaking into each other's ears. "I have no objection and I am very proud that you are so highly regarded by The Church, but Ses Theeth, I don't know about that," the Captain said as she crossed her arms over her chest and tapped innocently at her cheek with one finger. It was all part of the act and it seemed to Hiram that the crowd was buying it all.

The Captain went on. "So many powerful and influential women," she said feigning jealousy. She then leaned away from Hiram to act as if she were trying to talk to just the people in the crowd, her voice becoming both mocking and hinting at an element of truth at the same time. "And not all of those women are members of the Collective, if you know what I mean." She flashed a great smile and then approached Hiram again taking his hands. "Perhaps I need to send a chaperone with you, someone who can protect my interests." She released his hands and held her hands out to her sides indicating she was asking the whole crowd, "What do you think? Do I need to keep my future husband honest?"

Laughter erupted all around them, and by absolute luck one older woman raised her voice in a squeal saying, "He needs an Antodereo."

There were louder laughs.

"That might be a perfect idea," the Captain said.

Hiram knew that the Captain would have suggested it herself, if someone else hadn't, but at the same time he wondered if the old woman was in on the plan. He now noticed that although the woman wore a gold blouse and simple skirt (her clothing was, over all, less ostentatious than most guests) it was the color of her skirt that spoke volumes. It was forest green, the color of the Order of Saint Bridgid of the Sovereign Sisterhood.

Hiram pretended to not understand, as he had practiced.

"Antodereo, isn't that some sort of courtship matron?" he said. "I would not object to anything my darling's heart desired, and would accept this if you asked, but exactly what does it mean?"

"Sergeant Garchias come over here," the Captain called out into the crowd. People moved aside as the small woman made her way from the back of the crowd to come near the Captain and Hiram.

She had been in the crowd the whole time, watching, Hiram thought. He felt suddenly awkward and embarrassed and for a moment nearly forgot about the little play he was supposed to be a part of.

"Sergeant Tiranna Garchias as my personal assistant, and as a Sister in good standing, would you accept the responsibility of acting as my Antodereo and travel with my fiancé until he can return and we can be married?" the Captain said with a courteous bow and affectionate tone.

Tiranna snapped to attention, showing great flair and theatrical flourish for the crowds benefit, swirling her hand across her waist in a traditional gesture recognizing another person's nobility. "It would be my honor, and privilege to act in this regard for my lady, and my Captain," Tiranna said to calls of 'Bravo, bravo!' and 'Here, here!' from the crowd.

"Then it is all settled," the Captain said. "I couldn't feel better if I had you locked up in chains."

The general mood of the party continued to be light as people all around shared stories of the old courtship rituals told to them by their grandparents. People drifted away from Hiram, Tiranna, and the Captain, to enjoy the rest of the night's festivities.

Hiram whispered into the Captain's ear, "Even if they don't take it seriously, no one can deny you made your intentions clear."

The Captain gave him a worried look and whispered back, "Perhaps we didn't plan this right. I didn't think it would be looked at with as much humor as they showed. Oh well, we can just see how it goes."

For the next hour Tiranna followed close behind the Captain and Hiram as they went around the party meeting and exchanging pleasantries with many of the guests. They made every effort to demonstrate the seriousness of their engagement. Finally a few women approached the Captain and asked to speak to her in private, not in a serious way, but more in the way of married women who want to talk about wedding plans and receptions.

Hiram found himself in a group of very well dressed men, all older, maybe in their forties, each holding a tall glass of wine in one hand and a cigar in the other. Tiranna had stayed with Hiram, instead of going with the Captain, and it looked as though the test of the seriousness of her duties as Antodereo would be held right here and now.

"Young professor Whales, come here and have a cigar," said a portly, thin lipped man with a manicured mustache and small patch of hair on his chin. "We are just celebrating the second good news of the evening, Senator Rodrigo Thanteres has just been told his wife has delivered a daughter and mother and child are doing well."

A man standing close to the portly man stepped forward. He was very tall, and very broad shouldered, a near giant of a man. His head was bare of any hair at all, but he did not appear old, to Hiram. His skin was light reddish-brown and he had a clean, well shaved face. His chin was square and heavy, his brow prominent, and his nose had a distinctive slight bend right below his piercing blue eyes.

The large man held out a thick oversized cigar toward Hiram and introduced himself as he tried to make Hiram take the gift.

"Congratulations Mister Whales. I am Rodrigo Thanteres, Senator from the District of Culoota. We are fortunate men tonight, you and I. I have become a father, at last, and you shall soon be on the same path," the man's tone became suddenly suggestive and he winked at Hiram, "Wouldn't you agree my friend?"

The other men around them laughed deep in their throats, as Hiram took the cigar, and held it awkwardly, not knowing exactly what to do with it.

An elderly silver haired man with stooped shoulders came forward. Striking a large match and grinning he said, "Let me light that for you boy."

Hiram understood he needed to puff the cigar as the man held the match to it and found the smoke to be rather mild with slight hints of apple. The thing was obviously lit but the man kept the match at Hiram's face.

Tiranna stretched herself up onto her toes and whispered into Hiram's ear, "Roll the cigar around with your fingers until the whole end is burning."

Hiram gave a slight nod of understanding and did as she had instructed.

The gentlemen stood around and talked about the recent rise in the price of grains imported from the north, something Hiram didn't have much of an interest in.

He overheard one of the men say to Senator Rodrigo, "The lack of a central government makes it impossible to negotiate with those people. Every ship that comes into our ports wants to negotiate new trade arrangements and new prices for their wares. It is ridiculous."

Rodrigo stared at Hiram intently and then said, "What's your opinion professor. Do you share the opinion of my friend Edwarez? Do you think the people of Holdandun do not govern themselves wisely?"

Hiram knew quiet a bit about the clan structure of the Holdandun dwarves, but wondered if this senator was looking to get Hiram into a political argument to show off his own education. It was no secret that many senators were very well educated members of formerly noble or even royal families who at times were bitter about the change in the politics of Liegridan.

"There are definitely short comings to be evaluated in the clan structure of Holdandun," Hiram said. "But they have merits as well, and they have a strong history of cooperation among the clan leaders in the past when Holdandun was faced with problems affecting their country as a whole."

The men standing around made grim tight lipped nods of approval.

Hiram waited for the senator to rebut his comment, but was not prepared for the direction the big man took the conversation.

"How long have you lived on the university campus Mister Whales?"

Hiram did not miss the tone of the man's question, nor his decision to drop the use of the title of professor. Hiram suddenly began to worry he had stepped on the wrong toes. He needed to be diplomatic and respectful if he wanted to come out of this situation well. "I have lived on the campus for the last nine years," Hiram answered.

"And before that? Where does your family live Mister Whales?"

"My Family is spread out. My parents live in Goralda, My sisters and brothers are in Holdandun, and Anthandra. When I was twelve years old my parents sent me to the mission school in Los Rotavas. They always wanted me to be a priest, and I was pleased to fulfill my parent's wishes."

"So," Rodrigo said drawing the word out. "You must naturally believe it is best for women to rule the world."

It was a rude and rhetorical question. The men around them reacted with surprise, but none dared challenge or admonish the prominent senator.

Hiram took a moment to collect his thoughts. He wanted to be careful of what he said. Behind him he felt Tiranna nudge close and could sense her growing tension.

"I am fully aware that the conditions in this part of our world are not typical. I have been fortunate, even blessed to be brought up under the teachings of The Church at Ses Theeth. It would be difficult to argue that the over one million people who prosper under the laws set forth by the Council and approved in the Collective, do not agree with the conditions they find themselves in."

"Well said Mister Whales," Rodrigo said. "But tell me do you agree that it is better for your women to bury their men's heads in the sand and ignore the problems of their neighbors."

Tiranna was about to push past Hiram and confront the senator herself, but before she could a firm hand took her shoulder and held her back. The Captain had returned. Hiram did not know how much of the conversation she had overheard.

"Senator Rodrigo," the Captain said pleasantly. "It is good to see you again in this part of the country. I see you have met my fiancé. Hiram I hope the senator wasn't telling you terrible stories about the things he and his associates do while they are away from their wives."

A nervous man in the group said quickly, "We were just celebrating the birth of the senator's daughter, and your engagement Sister Rower."

"You company is always a pleasure," Rodrigo said to the Captain. "I was just waiting for Mister Whales to answer my question."

"I heard your question Senator," the Captain said. "I am surprised that you continue to try and frighten people with your notions of the terrible situation the country of Liegridan always seems to be in. Tell me what is it this year? Has the senate not been able to negotiate a fair price for trees cut down in Goralda, or maybe it is lemons this year from southern Anthandra?" She tried to add a bit of levity to her words, meaning not to directly insult the senator, but at the same time try and steer the argument away from politics.

The men around her were awkwardly, and very uncomfortably silent.

"Perhaps you haven't been told," Rodrigo said at last. "You and your women can think that the Senate of Liegridan is preoccupied with the cost of lettuce, but while you mock me right now thirty thousand soldiers in heavy armor with long bows and engines of war are making camp on the eastern shore of the river Yellin. In the past week our men have reported the movement of two separate columns of heavy cavalry, each well over ten thousand strong, moving across the plains of Hairen and toward Lake Dolores our south eastern border with Anthandra. The Prince of Goralda has cut off treaty negotiations and we have no guarantee of support from our Holdandun allies to the north. Anthandra is poised to invade. War is on the horizon. But you seem to think all we care about is trade. The attitude of your church and your sisterhood is appalling to me, like it has always been in the past. But mark my words Captain Rower. This time Anthandra will not simply claim another forty or fifty miles of our country as their own, no this time they will march right over us and right up to the gates of Ses Theeth, and then who will you turn to, to be your shield from the outside world."

"You've gone too far Rodrigo," the portly man said before the senator had finished. Other men in the group agreed and moved to put themselves between the Captain and the Senator.

"He's had too much to drink Sister," the elderly man said. "Forgive him his drunkenness. After all, he has a great event to celebrate and who can fault a man who is under so much stress when he lets himself go."

The Captain did not say a word but took Hiram's arm in hers and turned abruptly walking away without rushing, but not hiding her rising anger.

Tiranna stayed behind for a moment waiting to see if the senator would dare say anything further.

Before anything dangerous could happen, the Captain turned her head sharply and called out, "Sergeant you will get our carriage immediately."

Part 19

They walked briskly away from the party and as they passed by one of the small bon fires burning all around the perimeter of the tent the Captain turned and smiled, with some obvious difficulty, at Hiram. He was troubled and he knew she could tell.

"Hurry now and get the carriage," the Captain said to Tiranna who was coming up behind them. The young sergeant stopped, standing close to Hiram, and said.

"That was something you did back there."

"Tiranna do what I asked you," the Captain snarled, frightening Hiram just a little.

As Tiranna strode away, holding her fists balled and pressed into her thighs and leaning forward looking to all who could see as if she was on the verge of exploding into a rage, the Captain turned to Hiram and took notice of the strange look of disbelief on his face.

"Don't let the things the senator said make you troubled. He often speaks of things he only has limited real knowledge of. He is a hard man to deal with, but most of the time he is a good man."

Hiram moved close to the Captain and spoke quietly saying, "It's not that."

The Captain frowned and leaned her face close to Hiram's saying, "I hope you don't think I was keeping anything from you. I swear I have no idea what he is talking about. My work has been focused on this mission for weeks and anything he might say about the political situation is…"

Hiram interrupted her, "It isn't that either. I don't really want to talk about it."

He didn't want to damage the trust between them.

The Captain looked confused. "You should tell me what is bothering you. I promise not to judge you. I've been doing this sort of thing for most of my life and I can understand if it seems like I'm not bothered by the little hiccups we run into, but sometimes, Hiram I mean this, sometimes I get worried if I have done the right thing or not. Are you worried that you are making a mistake?"

"No, I mean, not really, but yes I have been thinking about that a lot the past few days. I keep thinking about Madame Dorchester, and how she just slipped away from us so fast and if it was because of anything I did, or didn't do, but that isn't what I'm, I mean what is bothering me right now is, I mean it's so silly, but I can't talk about it."

"Am I making you uncomfortable Hiram? Are you uncomfortable around me now because I kissed you?"

"No it isn't you," he said and turned away looking to see if the carriage was approaching.

"Oh, I see," the Captain said.

"No, it isn't what you think," he said and turned back quickly feeling he had offended her. In the near darkness this far from the fires at the festival he could just make out the curve of her eyes and the line of her cheek. He was captivated by her beauty. She had such a way of standing, just being next to her made him confused. He had feelings he didn't understand, feelings for Tiranna, and now feelings for the Captain he never expected to feel.

"Hiram, don't be ridiculous. It is exactly what I think it is. I'm old enough to be able to tell when a man is feeling attracted to a woman. I suppose it was to be expected that you might be attracted to the sergeant. She is a remarkable, talented, ferocious, and mysterious woman. In a lot of ways I guess she reminds me of me when I was younger, which is no secret among us and why I am so fond of her, not that I don't fully respect her talents you understand. She is raw, undisciplined, but eager and completely dedicated to her vows. And I guess I never thought to look at her in that way, she is rather small, but I suppose many men find that attractive. It is not a problem for me that you are attracted to her, and I don't think she is aware of how you feel. So unless you are planning to do something entirely bone headed, and against the plan we are executing here, I shouldn't think it would be a problem for you. Take a deep breath and remember what we are supposed to do."

"She hates me," Hiram said sounding like a lost child.

The Captain drew closer to Hiram and put her arms around his neck. To anyone watching from the festival tent it would appear the Captain and her fiancé were sharing an intimate moment. "Oh, come on now Hiram she doesn't hate you and I can say that with confidence. You are a very well respected scholar, a man who has shown a high degree of integrity and you are really not bad looking. Give her a chance to get to know you and who can say what will happen when all of this is finished."

"You really think she doesn't hate me," Hiram said with a little bit of disbelief.

"Oh no not at all," the Captain said as she moved a step away from him. The sound of the carriage wheels on the gravel roadway could be heard now.

"How can you be sure? I mean she acts like she hates me all of the time."

"Well, Hiram," she said just as the carriage came into view to their left. There were two small lamps hanging from the corners of the carriage roof lighting up the inside in a soft orange glow. The Captain turned to wait for the carriage to come to a stop and then turned her head around and winked at

Hiram whispering, "I'm pretty sure that if she really hated you she would have killed you all ready."

The carriage stopped right near them. The Captain opened the little half door and climbed in, holding it open for Hiram to join her with a large smile on her face.

Hiram had not really liked the Captain's little joke and then realizing he was keeping them waiting he decided to drop the subject and get into the carriage, this time sitting in the back next to the Captain, and said, "Of course what was I thinking."

Tiranna turned and glared at him with her mouth open and mumbled, "So annoying."

The Captain leaned into Hiram's neck and whispered again, mimicking his inflection perfectly, "Of course, she still might."

Tiranna snapped the reigns and the carriage took off at a quick pace. When they were well beyond the hearing range of the festival, and still in the open spaces before coming back into the neighborhoods of the western part of the city the Captain said, "Sergeant take me to the twelfth street mission and then return the carriage to the reverend mother's coach house. Then I want the both of you to go straight back to the apartment. We may have to accelerate our plans again. Don't go anywhere in the morning until you hear from me or the High Priestess."

"Back to the apartment, what do you mean?" Hiram asked.

"Your things were moved into Tiranna's apartment near the beach while we were at the festival," the Captain said as she began to unlace her bodice. "I meant to tell you about it when I picked you up but we got to talking about the shoes and I forgot. You will be staying with Tiranna until you leave. You will be on sabbatical starting tomorrow. As soon as I inform her holiness what has been spoken of tonight I'm certain she will agree that we should get you going to Ses Theeth immediately. I will send out messages to our officers in the eastern regions and see what intelligence we can gather before you depart." She finished unlacing the black bodice and threw it onto the seat next to her. Her body heaved with a deep breath and she reached behind her head to remove the leather barrette from her hair. "Don't look like that," she said to Hiram. "There isn't any reason to panic, yet. We have a few days before a passage can be arranged for the two of you going west. We will have to acquire some supplies and necessary equipment for the both of you. We may even," She stopped in mid sentence, and then said sternly to Hiram, "Stop looking at me that way."

Tiranna turned to see what was causing the Captain to say what she had said, and the sergeant, seeing Hiram's mouth and eyes wide open, turned her head slightly further around to see what he was staring at and then broke out laughing.

The Captain looked down at her chest, which had almost escaped the top of her dress when she violently removed her bodice. Her ample bosom was the focus of Hiram's stare.

"Oh you are both so immature," the Captain growled quickly adjusting her parts back down into her dress. "You," she yelled at the sergeant, "Keep your eyes on the road. And you, Mister Whales, if we weren't formally engaged I would slap your face." She tried to maintain a sense of sternness, but found herself giving into laughter she couldn't control.

They were quiet for the rest of the ride into the city where the Captain was dropped off at the Mission of the Sisters of the Blessed Flame. It was a small wooden building along a street filled with shops and cafes.

"How will you get home?" Tiranna asked.

"I will stay here tonight," the Captain said getting out of the carriage. "I have a lot of letters to write. I will try to come to see you first thing in the morning, probably after I meet with the High Priestess and the reverend mother. Don't wait for us if you are hungry, go ahead and eat in the morning, but don't leave the apartment. Good night Sergeant," she said and then absent mindedly leaned back over the small carriage door and kissed Hiram lightly on the lips, "Good night Hiram."

She hurried into the building, which was not locked, and Tiranna called the horses to get moving again. She pulled the team into a tight turn in the middle of the road and then whipped them gently to make them trot away at a fast pace.

As the carriage moved quickly down the road Hiram got up off of the back seat and put his knees on the cushioned seat at the front of the carriage behind and below the driver's seat.

"Why did she do that?" he asked Tiranna.

"Do what?" she answered.

"She kissed me when she said good bye. Why did she do that?"

"She is your fiancée she can kiss you if she wants to."

"We aren't really engaged," he tried to sound authoritative.

"Yes you are," she said mockingly.

"Not really."

"Yes really. You don't have to marry her, that is your choice, but for all purposes you are really, really engaged, and it would help the matter, GREATLY, if you tried to act like you understand that."

"But I thought…" he tried to think of the right thing to say.

"Oh you thought, seriously, you thought? You thought what exactly? No don't tell me. It's probably best if you don't try and explain. I can take only so many, 'of courses' in one day. You should sit down I'm going to get the team going a little faster. We have to get back soon. I have things I need to do tonight."

"What is so wrong with saying, 'of course'? It is a respectable way of showing a person that you understand them."

"You say it all the time, and the way you say it, it sounds more condescending than respectable."

"Really?" Hiram said astonished.

"Yes, really," Tiranna answered and snapped the reigns hard enough to make the horse jump, and Hiram was thrown backward into the back carriage seat.

Part 20

After returning the carriage, Hiram and Tiranna started the long walk to her apartment.

It was well into night, but the moon was fuller than it had been on the night Hiram had gone to the North Tower and first learned of the mission he was about to undertake.

"How far away is your apartment?" Hiram asked as they left the universities carriage house near the reverend mother's residence.

"About half a mile," Tiranna answered.

They walked in silence. Hiram did not walk next to the sergeant, but instead walked just behind her. When Hiram could hear waves crashing on the beach he asked, "You have a place this close to the shore?"

"It was the Captain's idea," she replied.

The building where Tiranna's apartment was located had once been a three story mansion. It was built fifty years ago by Juan and Hurina Dargez and was one of the oldest buildings on the street. The street, a bricked paved avenue that ran parallel to the shore for a few hundred yards before turning to the south, was built up over the years with small bungalows and boat cottages (very small shacks with an attached three sided building that could shelter a small boat. These small boats, generally less than ten feet long were kept on two wheeled carts, the wheels where made from soft woods making the carts light and easy to pull across the sandy beach).

The beach north of the street was wide, and rose up in a pleasant low dune before dropping back down into the waters of the Ses Mar (the bay between the peninsula of Theeth and the southern coast of Holdandun). At high tide the waters nearly reached to top of the dune and when rare storms came into the bay water would crest over the dune and threaten the houses and buildings along the road. But mostly those rare storms were driven by easterly winds and little serious damage had ever been done to the north shore villages of Las Rotavas.

Tiranna's apartment building, the old Dargez mansion, was on the south side of the rode and her apartment was on the third floor. Behind the building was a narrow alleyway separating the buildings on the south side of the road from a row of single story houses built just in the last few years. For many years people did not want to move to this side, the west side, of Las Rotavas because no fresh water wells could be found. Just after the Dargez mansion was built (which had a large fresh water cistern built into the basement that stored collected rain water from the roof drains) engineers from the city completed a fresh water aqueduct that ran a full thirteen miles from the hills in the south east into Las Rotavas, and then they installed underground pipes made of baked clay to bring water out to the edges of the city (as much as a mile away from the city center at the estuary of the small river Rotavas). The city had been growing steadily ever since and was becoming one of the largest cities in western Liegridan.

"You have to keep your voice down until we get inside," Tiranna said as she began ascending a wooden staircase attached to the west side of the large building. "The tenants on the first two floors will complain if we are too loud."

The stairs rose to the second floor, at the southwest corner, and then they had to cross a covered walkway that went from the southwest corner of the building to the southeast corner where a second stair, this one crossing the east face, rose up to the third floor. There was a wide and partially covered veranda almost as wide as the whole north face of the building where the stairs ended, with large fat clay flower pots in the corners and two over sized chairs made from the woven soft bark of the palm trees that grew wild all along the beaches from here to Costa Delgarmo. There was a single door in the center of the veranda, and to the west of this, past a space on the wall where the veranda ended and there was a gap of about five feet, was a second veranda, uncovered with a similar and smaller door.

Hiram whispered to Tiranna, "How do those people get to their apartment?" pointing at the door to the west. "I don't see any stairs."

"That's the main bedroom of my apartment," Tiranna said as she opened the door in front of her and entered the apartment. "I used to use it as a practice room but I had to move my things out when they said you would be moving in with me. There is a bed and a desk in there now for you to use. You can open the doors during the day," she was saying as she crossed the room that was the main part of the apartment to a high round table where a brass ornamental oil lamp sat. She lit the lamp with a match drawn from a short wooden cup behind the lamp and went on, "The breezes are gentle and it cools the room down so it isn't uncomfortable at night, but I have to insist that you close and lock the doors at night before you sleep. The roof of the building is easily accessible and anyone can drop down onto the veranda from the overhang above."

She adjusted the wick of the lamp and then attached a polished brass plate to one side of it. The room was brightened enough for Hiram to make out all of the details fairly well.

It was a big room, probably intended for gathering a large family for meals, but there was almost no furniture. Against the east wall were two wardrobes, and between them a set of low hooks were mounted on the wall. To his right there was a little desk and chair. There was an opening in the wall next to the desk that was wide enough for two people to pass through. Beyond this opening Hiram could see the end of a large bed. In the south wall was a similar opening and the space beyond that was apparently a kitchen.

"They must not have been fond of doors," Hiram said as he walked toward the bedroom on his right. The room that must have been the one she said was now his.

"No, and I like it," Tiranna said. "You can open the patio doors there, and the window in the back room, the bath room, and the wind just blows right through." She took a deep breath, "The air is always fresh, and the smell of the sea is very nice."

The light from Tiranna's lamp cast long shadows into the bedroom beyond the opening. Hiram noticed the large size of the bedroom, and the bed, which was easily twice the size of the bed in his dormitory room on campus. Even the desk was large, and it had a rolling cover. Near the desk were two large trunks with wide leather straps and a small wooden open topped box.

"Where will you be sleeping?" Hiram asked as he turned around.

Tiranna was not there. The lamp was sitting on the table casting its light across the apartment.

He walked toward the kitchen of the apartment and heard Tiranna's voice coming from a room that was through the kitchen and to the right.

"This is my room," she said from where he could not see her. "Just wait out there and I will show you the bathroom, and how to use the pump and the water heater. I just need to change first and get out of this uniform. There's some fruit on the table next to the basin in the kitchen. Help yourself."

After a short time she came out into the kitchen and closed the door behind her. She had changed into a very tight fitting black garment that covered her from neck to ankles. Hiram had never seen a woman dressed in this way before. Every curve of her body was revealed. Hiram remembered how when she had handed him his letters he had thought she was fifteen or sixteen years old, but now it was obvious she was a full grown woman. She walked passed him, reaching out to push him gently with her right forearm as she passed.

"My room has a door. We just installed it, but I'm afraid I will have to keep it open when we are sleeping, unless you are grown up enough to be comfortable with me sleeping in your room," she said as she crossed the kitchen toward another door in the east wall. She opened the door and went into the mostly dark room saying, "This is the bathroom, with plumbing no less. When you have to go just be clean about it, and pull this chain when you are finished. Water from that box near the ceiling will flush the bowl. Then," she said moving to a sink under a window with a strange looking apparatus next to it at the opposite end of the little room. She lifted what looked like a long handle and moved it up and down. Water came out of a pipe near the sink and she said, "Wash your hands in the water before it can drain. There is soap in the dish on the window sill right here. When you are done washing your hands close this valve, open this one, and pump the handle four or five times. That puts more water in the tank. Make sure you shut the valve you opened when you are done, and if you want a hot bath," she reached under the sink and retrieved a large wooden bucket. "Open this valve again, pump like this to fill the bucket, and then fill this tank next to the tub." Tiranna spoke quickly and moved around the room touching things he didn't recognize or understand. "There is a fire box down here. I will check it regularly to make sure it has the right amount and size of wood for the fire. When the water is hot you can open this valve and the hot water will fill the tub. Don't worry about forgetting the fire. If the water gets too hot it vents out of a pipe to the outside as steam, but be careful. If you let it get too hot you will have to pump more water from the sink into the bucket and mix cold water with the hot water until it is cooled enough to take a bath."

Tiranna was being very thorough about the instructions for the very modern equipment. Hiram waited until it seemed she was finished and then asked, "In my bed?"

"What? Tiranna said dumbfounded.

"You said if I was grown up enough to let you sleep in my bedroom. Did you mean in the bed, in the bed with me?" it was impossible for him to conceal his nervousness.

"Were you listening to what I was telling you about the water, the hot water tank, the pump, did you get all that?"

Hiram walked around the room and touched each device and repeated, word for word, everything Tiranna had said. She stared at him with a strange look, and Hiram wondered if she was impressed at how accurately he remembered each and every little thing.

When he finished repeating the instructions and the safety warning of the bath tub, he turned to her and said again, "In my bed?"

She didn't say anything for a moment and Hiram grew even more nervous.

Finally she said as she pushed past him for the second time in just a few minutes, "Of course not in your bed. I can sleep on the floor, which is probably the best thing to do."

Hiram laughed a little laugh and smiled.

"Now what?" Tiranna asked stopping in the kitchen and turning around to face him. Hiram came very close to her and looked down into her face.

"You just said 'of course'."

She spun away from him and said, "You should get some sleep. I have some routines I must do before I turn in. If you are asleep when I'm finished I will try not to disturb you, but I will bring a few blankets and a pillow into your room and sleep on the floor. Do you understand?"

"Of...I mean yes I understand, and thank you sergeant for taking such good care of me. I hope I can repay your kindness someday," he said.

He hurried to move past her and was particular about gently touching her upper arm with his hand, in a gesture similar to her pushing him out of her way with her arm, and said, "Excuse me please."

As he left the kitchen and crossed the main room toward the large bedroom he thought he heard the sound of a foot stamping hard on the wooden floor behind him.

Part 21

Tiranna wanted to punch that man's face in. He was so incredibly pompous and smug. Oh she saw right through his innocent and shy act, and she knew that he was no better than any other man she had ever met.

But he did remember everything she had said in the bathroom, and he was always very respectful of the Captain, right up until he practically fell over himself in the cab. She calmed down as he past through the large room and she kept her eyes on him until he was out of sight in the bedroom.

"I have exercises to do so if you don't need anything else I would appreciate it if you tried not to bother me for the next couple of hours," she called after him raising her voice just slightly.

"No I'll be fine I just need to get out of this suit. Hey, what are these trunks in here for?" he called back from the other room.

She hurried across the room to the open doorway between the two rooms all the while making a shushing noise. "You can't be that loud," she said as she came to a stop unconsciously before crossing the threshold into the man's bedroom. He was standing by the two trunks. She could just barely make out his outline in the darkness. "Just a minute stay right there."

She went and got the lamp from the tall table in the main room and this time entered into the bedroom and placed the lamp on the large desk. As she did she noticed he had removed his shoes and the dress coat. The shoes he wore were placed neatly at the foot of the bed and the jacket was folded small and set on top of the bed above where he had placed the shoes.

"You're very neat," she said trying not to look at him.

"Thank you and I'm sorry about the shouting. I'll be quieter."

He walked past her, between her and the lamp and she was able to see through the thin material of the silk shirt he wore. He was wearing another shirt under that one, which she thought was odd. He went to the small set of doors at the north end of the room, having to pass around the large bed.

Lifting two separate latches he opened the doors and stepped out onto the veranda beyond. The moon shone on the water and he could hear the rolling crashes of the waves against the shore.

"It's a beautiful view," Hiram said.

He turned around just as she turned to look toward him. He was silhouetted in the silvery moonlight. She noticed he was slimmer, even slimmer than she originally thought he was. All of the times she had seen him in his robes so many times before he had looked a little dumpy in the middle, but in the tight suit pants and tucked in silk shirt he was positively thin.

"Well, um," she said. "I'm going to be exercising now so, yes, just remember to close and lock the door before you uh retire."

He came back around the bed with a puzzled look on his face. "The trunks," he said. "What are they for?"

"Oh, yes, well. Those have your clothes, from your room, and the box has the things that were on and in your desk," she said.

"Oh, alright," Hiram said as he began to unbutton his shirt.

She realized she was staring at his hands when he said, "Do you mind? Don't you have some exercising to do?"

She snapped her eyes away from him and left the room.

Crossing the big room she inhaled and exhaled with force, driving her mind to be clear of any distractions, and launched herself forward into a routine and well practiced flip aiming her feet for the hooks in the wall. Her pacing was off and her feet struck the wall too low, and her flip carried her onto her rear, landing in a heap in the corner where the wall met the floor with a loud thump.

Looking back across the floor of the room, upside down, she saw him come to the doorway with a concerned look.

"Are you all right? Is that supposed to happen?" He said. He had removed his dress shirt and the undershirt he wore had no sleeves and was cut low around his neck His shoulders though not large were square and muscular. His waist was so impossibly narrow for a man of leisure.

She felt her face flush in embarrassment. "NO, I mean YES!" she raised her voice. "Yes that is exactly what is supposed to happen." She rolled over her shoulders and sprang to her feet shaking her body all over and tipping her head to each side slowly stretching her muscles.

"Oh all right, well good night, and be careful," Hiram said and turned around, then he turned back suddenly and whispered, "And try to be quiet."

Tiranna ran in place for several seconds and then let out a physical scream, as she had been taught to do when the tension in the body is reaching a peak.

She began a series of vaults, head over heals, landing each time as quietly as she could. She practiced a few without letting her hands touch the ground, and then she tried a few variations, spreading her legs in an inverted split while tumbling with only one hand. She moved across the floor quickly from wall to wall, gaining speed and momentum as she did. She forced herself to close her eyes and focus her mind on her memory of the room's dimensions. She had done these routines thousands of times, and she would not be distracted tonight.

"I will count the pillars of faith and recite the prayers of each cardinal coordinate," she was saying in her mind as the tension fell away from her.

She had worked into a rhythm that was honing her body and clearing her mind when she heard his voice suddenly saying, "What are these things?"

She opened her eyes, while in the middle of an inverted vault, just in time to see her feet strike him right in the face.

He was knocked backward, with his arms (which had been carrying two bundles) flying upward throwing the bundles into the air. She completely lost her focus and tumbled out of control to land on top of him (with her back against his chest). She opened her mouth to say, "What in the hells are you doing?" when the bundles came back down and struck her on the face right below her left eye, her bad eye.

"Owwee!" she exclaimed. Then rolled off of Hiram and said harshly, "You moron can't you see I was…" She stopped when she realized he had been knocked unconscious.

Tiranna went into a shaking fit. "Oh, God of the Vapors I've killed him!" she cried.

"No, no don't panic, sergeant, don't panic, check his pulse first." She was talking out loud in a staccato tremble. She put her hand against his chest. It was warm and she felt a light growth of hair that until now she hadn't noticed. Hiram's chest rose and fell in a steady peaceful tempo and Tiranna rocked back onto her heels sitting next to him and heaved a heavy sigh.

The bundles he had been carrying were a small stack of books tied together with heavy string, and a multi-unit assembly of leather pouches with individual closable flaps with buckles made of silver.

Something warm was running down her left cheek. She reached up and felt a trickle of blood.

Tiranna stood up suddenly and rushed to the bathroom, remembering the injury she had received so many years ago and how they had told her she was so lucky that she did not lose her eye. She flung open the bathroom window, letting in just a faint amount of moon and star light. There was a small handheld polished glass mirror on the counter next to the sink and she took it and held it up by her face while standing near the window.

It was just a small cut, just below her eye, and it had already stopped bleeding. She pumped some water into the basin and splashed it onto her face. Putting her hands against the cold marble of the basin she tried to calm her nerves, looked at her face in the mirror again, and for no reason that she understood at all she began to cry.

"Stop it, stop it, stop it," she gritted through her teeth. Then she stood as straight as she could, took a deep breath and said out loud to herself, "You are a sergeant in the Sovereign Sisterhood and will not fall to pieces. Do you understand me girl!"

She shook off her mixed and confused feelings, wet a towel, taken from where it was draped on the edge of the bath tub, and rushed back to where Hiram lay on the floor.

He was still out.

Putting down the wet cloth she lifted him, he was light enough for her to manage easily, and put him down on the side of the bed. She reached across him and pulled down the light blanket and cotton sheet and then rolled Hiram over into the spot she had uncovered. She ran around the foot of the bed and came to the other side with her back to the patio door. He was still wearing his suit pants but she pulled the covers up over him anyway trying not to even think about whether she should undress him or not.

She remembered the towel, retrieved it from the floor and touched it to his forehead. Then she began speaking in a soft soothing voice to try and discover if he could hear her.

"Hiram, Hiram can you hear me? It's Tiranna I'm so sorry I hit you. It was a complete accident. Hiram, Hiram?"

He stirred and tried to open his eyes. "OhhhhWow, my head," he groaned and reached up to put his hand against his eyes. His hand instead struck Tiranna's who was still gently wiping his face with the wet cloth. Reflexively she dropped the cloth and took his hand in hers.

Hiram smiled and closed his eyes, squeezing Tiranna's hand gently.

Tiranna's heart nearly stopped beating, and then began to race in a way she never felt before. It made her afraid, and angry, but she couldn't let go of his hand. She began to tremble, and then she couldn't understand why she was fighting off another bout of tears, then she felt fine, and then it started all over again.

She didn't know what to do, or what to say, and realized that for the first time in her life she wasn't sure of what she was feeling. She tried to just breathe, and watch his face, wanting to leave him, but not wanting to leave. He fell asleep like that, still holding her hand.

The doors behind her were still open. He hadn't closed them like she reminded him to do and that made her angry again. The night air was growing cooler, and the sound of the waves came and went in different intensities. The sound rolled around her head and lulled her into a sleep she didn't know she needed.

Part 22

Someone was knocking lightly on the apartment door.

Tiranna woke feeling disoriented. She was sleeping on the floor next to the large bed in Hiram's room. There was light coming in under the doors to the veranda. The doors were closed. She didn't remember closing them. She quietly crawled away from the bed toward the main room, and then tip-toed to the front door.

She tried to open the door but found it was locked, and she didn't remember doing that either. Releasing the latch and sliding back the second lock bolt she opened it slowly readying her body for anything unusual by taking a deep slow breath.

A woman was at the door. She looked very much like Madame Dorchester, but younger by a few years. She wore a simple brown dress and a black cloth was tied over her head and around her chin covering her hair. In her hands in front of her was a folded grey heavy garment.

"Is Mister Whales here?" the woman asked.

"Why would a Mister Whales be here?" Tiranna said. She was suspicious of this strange woman, but not ready to go on the offensive immediately. "This is my apartment. I live here."

The woman looked at her strangely, and then smiled and said, "They told me at the university that Hiram Wales was staying in this apartment I'm sorry I bothered you."

Tiranna stepped out through the door making the woman back up a step. Then she closed the door quietly behind her. It was cool and bright out on the veranda and the sun was barely over the mountains in the east.

"Who at the university told you Mister Whales was in this apartment?" Tiranna asked as she folded her arms across her stomach and studied the old woman carefully.

"A priestess of some authority I believe. I asked for someone who could put me in touch with Hiram Whales, on behalf of my sister, and a young woman named Doreen sent me to see a woman named Marjory Dalinas. I spoke with her about the matter of my sister's will and she said I could find Hiram here."

"You are Madame Dorchester's sister?"

"Yes my name is Maureen Dorchester. I'm sorry to trouble you, but did you say Hiram Whales was not here?" The old woman again gave Tiranna a strange look.

"What exactly is your business with Mister Whales?" Tiranna asked.

"Who are you, if you don't mind my asking," the old woman said.

"My name is Tiranna Garchias. I am currently responsible for all appointments for Mister Whales. I was not told he would be having visitors. I hope you understand I have to be very careful about doing my job."

"Miss Garchias," the woman said. "These things belonged to my sister and she left instructions in her will that they should be given to Mister Whales. If you would give them to him for me I will consider my work complete." Her voice became very curt, and she handed the grey folded garment to Tiranna. "Good day Miss Garchias," the woman finished, turned and took the stairs leaving the apartment veranda.

Tiranna waited and watched the woman leave until she turned the corner at the bottom of the stairs. She looked to the left and right before opening the door and going back into the apartment. Hiram was just coming out of the bedroom into the main room. It was shadowy, and the only light in the room was coming in from the open front door. She left the door open, and came into the main room.

Hiram stayed at the opening between the two rooms and said, "Who was that?"

"A woman saying she was Madame Dorchester's sister dropped off these things. She said her sister left them to you in her will," Tiranna said as she placed the garment on the floor.

Hiram came away from the shadowy bedroom and into the light of the main room and Tiranna saw the bruises under his eyes and all across his nose.

"Oh my," Tiranna gasped.

Just then Hiram, who was approaching Tiranna, stopped and peered at her face saying, "What happened to you."

"What are you talking about?" Tiranna said.

"You have a black eye and a cut right here," he said and lightly touched Tiranna on the cheek.

"I had an accident last night," Tiranna said innocently, and then found it hard to ask, "How are you feeling?"

"I have a terrible pain right in the front of my brain," Hiram said.

"I should probably explain that."

Part 23

The Captain had much to think about when she entered the mission building. There were two sisters on duty there that night, Sister Ganime and Sister Rosalinda. They were both privates in the Sisterhood of Saint Bridgid, young women. It took nearly till past midnight for the Captain to write four copies of a letter explaining her concerns about the rumors of troop movements and the threat of war mentioned by the Senator. The letters were given to Sister Rosalinda with instructions to deliver them to the missions in Galidi, Foremosa, and Santa Yalerra. The forth letter was given to Sister Ganime and she was told to take it directly to the reverend mother of the university (the forth letter contained an extra request for the revered mother to send the High Priestess Marjory Dalinas to come to sergeant Garchias' apartment in the morning as soon as she could make it). The Captain then instructed Sister Ganime to go to her house, on the south side of the city, and collect a change of clothing for her. The Captain would sleep in the mission tonight, and then go straight to Sergeant Garchias' apartment in the morning. Sister Ganime would be at least three hours traveling to the university, the Captain's house and then back to the mission. Those three hours were all the sleep the Captain would have.

She slept uneasy, in a cot in the upstairs barracks of the mission, a place normally kept clean and ready for any people down on their fortunes needing shelter and then rose early before the sun. Her dress, from the party the night before, was her blanket. When she rose she found the clothing Sister Ganime left for her on the floor at the foot of the cot. She dressed quickly and started out for the west end of the city, hoping to reach the apartment before the sunrise.

The Captain was stopped several times, in the street, by people wanting to congratulate her on the announcement of her engagement. The idea that what she had done, even if it had been something she knew was only important to ensure the sergeant could travel without question with Hiram, started to bother her. It had never occurred to her how significant this sort of thing was to the regular people of Las Rotavas. She tried to be cordial to each and every stranger that stopped her, becoming a bit overwhelmed by the idea that something that was said at a party the night before, in front of a few dozen people of the city, could spread around so quickly. It was as if everyone had nothing else to talk about. When she finally reached the apartment building it was well past sun up.

She went up the stairs quickly and when she reached the veranda of Tiranna's apartment and noticed the door was open she became nervous. She approached the door slowly, heard Hiram's and Tiranna's voice in the room just beyond the door and relaxed. She walked in through the open door of the apartment and stopped as soon as she saw

Hiram, who was facing her, and exclaimed, "Hiram what happened to you."

She rushed past Tiranna to take Hiram's head in her hands. "Are you all right? How did this happen? Where you attacked?"

Hiram was startled and was about to say something when the Captain turned suddenly away from him to face Tiranna.

"Sergeant, explain how…" the Captain began harshly and then saw Tiranna's bruise and small cut. "Who did this? How many of them were there? Did you leave any bodies in the street," the Captain seemed less angry, but was feverishly asking questions when Tiranna finally interrupted her and said.

"It was an accident. I kicked him in the face, and he dropped some strange bundles on me."

The Captain stared in disbelief for a moment and then took Tiranna by the arms and said, "You kicked him in the face?"

Hiram peered out from behind the Captain and repeated the question, "You kicked me in the face?"

"It was an accident. I was exercising and he came in the room and I didn't see him in time to stop and we collided. It was a complete accident."

"I think I remember you coming at me. You were upside down," Hiram said.

"Yes it was a complete accident," Tiranna said.

There was silence for a long while and the Captain finally released Tiranna.

"Sergeant go and change," the Captain said. "The High Priestess will be arriving soon and we have serious business to attend to. What is this?" she asked pointing at the grey bundle on the floor.

Tiranna was already walking away but said over her shoulder, "Some kind of inheritance from Madame Dorchester to Hiram. Her sister dropped it off just before you arrived."

"That's impossible," the Captain said and carefully stepped back away from the bundle pulling Hiram with her.

Tiranna stopped before reaching the kitchen and turned around.

Hiram moved closer to the Captain and said, "What do you mean?"

"Madame Dorchester left all of her things to the Sisterhood, and I happen to know that her sister, her natural sister, isn't in the city."

"I saw her sister at the funeral," Hiram said. "She was here just a week ago."

"And she left the day after the funeral," the Captain said. We have been tracking the passenger manifests of every ship leaving and arriving in Las Rotavas since the night the Eysturlun was killed. Tiranna go ahead and change, and then tell me about this sister of Madame Dorchester's."

While Tiranna changed the Captain examined Hiram's bruises. He kept telling her he didn't feel as bad as she was telling him it looked. "Can you breathe without any difficulty?" she asked.

"Yes I feel fine. Except for a slight headache is all." He told her.

"I want you to go lie down until Marjory arrives. The sergeant can tell me about the woman who was here. By the way did you see her?"

"No, she was gone before I got out of bed. I heard the door open and came in here just as Tiranna was bringing those things in from outside."

"All right, go lay down. We can't take any changes with you possibly having a concussion. I want Marjory to examine you thoroughly."

Tiranna came back into the room after Hiram had left to return to his bed.

"The woman that came here said she spoke to the High Priestess. I had no reason to be suspicious, and didn't sense anything evil about her," Tiranna said carefully approaching the bundle.

"That's good to know, but not everyone who might want to see this mission fail will be evil," The Captain said. "Was there anything else about her that you can remember?"

"She kept looking at me in an awkward way. Let me think," Tiranna was saying as a shadow was cast through the doorway.

"I came as quickly as I could. What happened?" It was the High Priestess, who was dressed in commoner's attire, no official robes, or colors to identify her. Her usually long and combed hair was put up in a hasty bun on the top of her head.

"I need to tell you what I learned last night at the festival," the Captain said. "Everything went fine as far as the announcement was concerned, but while I was away from Hiram I heard some disturbing news, and Senator Rodrigo had some things to say as well that I think you will find important. Before that though, I need you to check on Hiram." The Captain took Marjory by the arm and pulled her as she hurried into Hiram's room. Tiranna followed close behind.

"Sergeant open those doors and let more light in here," the Captain said.

When the doors were flung open the Captain and the High Priestess where standing with their backs to the veranda and Tiranna.

The High Priestess inhaled sharply when the light fell across Hiram's face.

"What happened?" she said as she bent over and peered, without touching, at the bruises on Hiram's nose.

"There was some sort of accident last night," the Captain said.

Marjory looked cross at the Captain, and then rose up and turned toward Tiranna saying, "How did this happen?"

"It was a complete accident," Tiranna was saying when the High Priestess crossed the floor to come closer to her.

Marjory took Tiranna's chin in her hand and examined her face as well, then a sly smile came over her lips and she turned back to the Captain and said, "An accident."

"That's what she said," the Captain repeated becoming annoyed.

Marjory came back to the bed and smiled down at Hiram. "Was this your 'first' accident Hiram?"

"That's not funny," the Captain and Tiranna said simultaneously.

Marjory had to laugh, and then said, "I'm sorry that was rude. How do you feel Hiram?"

"I feel fine," he said timidly, "Just a little headache."

"How did you get the cut sergeant?" Marjory asked without turning away from Hiram.

"A buckle from some kind of pack Hiram was carrying. When I kicked him it went into the air and when it fell it hit me on the cheek."

Hiram suddenly sat up in bed and said, "Yes I remember now. I was asking Tiranna what those things were, the stack of books and strange bags, when she kicked me in the face."

"You kicked him in the face?" Marjory said.

"She kicked him in the face," sighed the Captain.

"Yes! I kicked him in the face. I'm sorry. It was an accident, a complete accident. Do we have to keep mentioning that?" Tiranna exclaimed.

Hiram slid across the bed and leaned over to the floor away from the side the three women were standing by and recovered the two packages.

"These," he said.

"How did you get those?" Marjory asked. "I've been looking for those since the night at the north tower at the university."

"You left them in my apartment when we all followed Tiranna that night," Hiram said. "I tried to return them once, but things got so complicated."

"They are important Hiram," the High Priestess said taking them from his hands.

She untied the string around the books. There were three of them. One of them was larger than the other two, and it was a regular looking sort of book with a dusty brown leather cover. The other two were smaller books and had covers in bright embossed leather that wrapped all around the book, keeping the pages completely sealed inside of them. One of the smaller books was blue and the other was a creamy white.

"This," Marjory said handing the large brown book back to Hiram, "Is a blank journal and I want you to use this every chance you have to record your observations, notes on events, and any information you discover while on your mission. These," she added holding up the other two books, "Are your prayer books and contain the prayers you need to cast the most common spells needed by a traveling cleric."

"Prayer, books?" Hiram asked. "Aren't spell prayers normally kept on individual scrolls?"

"The traditional methods for learning the prayers have been reliable and proven for as long as anyone can remember," the High Priestess said as she turned her body slightly and sat on the edge of the bed next to Hiram. "There were always little difficulties, and often some disagreement about the order and power of certain spells young clerics were taught. Then," she opened the blue leather book and began showing it to Hiram, "A system was suggested that ordered the spells by their complexity and effects and this idea was put into use, creating these new prayer guides, you might call them."

Hiram was looking at the pages in the book when his eye went wide and he gasped, "That's my system!"

"Yes," Marjory said smiling broadly, "It is. And it has shown itself to be a very good system."

"But," Hiram was trying to say as he took the book into his own hands, "I got into so much trouble when that paper was published. Only the pleading of Madame Dorchester kept my out of a trial for heresy."

"That was some time ago Hiram," Marjory said. "Yes there were some in The Church who were troubled by your observations and your ideas about classifying the various divine spells, but in a very short time after that paper was read before the Collective it was agreed that the system could be of great benefit to our efforts in work abroad. Having books such as these, with the prayers set down in logical order, and with the notes that were added by some of the best teachers of The Church canon set down in each section with the prayers that make those spells accessible, has turned out to be one the most significant steps forward for us in hundreds of years. This blue book contains the prayers for all unprotected spells that you classified in the first to third level of power. The prayers are simple to read, and any necessary somatic or material component requirements are written in the margins for clarification. The white book contains a small selection of prayers, ones that are felt to be common and likely to be needed by a priestess who is away from a large mission, from your classifications of forth and fifth level. These are somewhat powerful spells and it is not uncommon for the divine spirit of Xetas to choose not to grant his power for their use. However, the explanatory notes are much longer in the white book, and it is hoped that a priestess," she was then interrupted by the Captain.

"Or priest."

"Yes, or priest," Marjory went on, "Will understand the importance of the order and prayer devotion required to be granted access to these divine spells."

"Prayer books," Hiram said. "That's incredible, and using my system. I don't know what to say. How are they? I mean do the priestesses have trouble using them?"

"I haven't heard anyone say they are not happy that they have these books," Marjory said now standing up and placing the books on Hiram's lap, "And now you can tell us, yourself, when you return if they were helpful to you."

"These are mine?" Hiram asked.

"Yes and the component pouch as well," Marjory said.

"Component pouch?" Hiram asked.

"This bag like item," Marjory said picking up the leather pouches. "It is a custom component pouch. They're very popular with clerics who spend most of their time on the road, away from a safe place to keep various spell components. There are eleven separate pouches and they are connected by straps and buckles so that it can be arranged as the user sees fit. The two largest pouches are divided inside into five separate pockets each for very small items. The component pouch can be worn as a belt or as a shoulder bag. Now it isn't large enough to carry every component needed to cast every spell that requires a component, but it can carry the most common and needed components for emergency situations."

"I'm going to need to cast spells? Is that what you are saying?" Hiram asked as he scooted a bit away from the High Priestess.

"Well to use you own words Hiram, of course."

Part 24

The three women exchanged nervous glances.

"Is there some reason why you wouldn't cast spells if you needed to Hiram?" The Captain asked.

"I thought you said he was ordained," Tiranna said to no one in particular.

Marjory turned a frown toward the sergeant and said, "Sergeant Garchias I hope this continued disrespect of Hiram is going to cease soon."

"Hiram," Marjory turned to him and then said, "Please forgive the sergeant. She still has much to learn about how the future of the Sovereign Sisterhood and The Church at Ses Theeth are dependent on each other. You are not concerned about using divine magic in public are you? You are far from the first man to do so, you know. It has become quiet common, and in most of the rest of the world there are priest and priestesses following the callings of their faith in every culture."

"No," Hiram said. "It isn't that I'm afraid." He moved off of the bed away from the women, to stand on the opposite side. "It's just that I never have, actually, cast a spell myself."

"You've lived at the university for nine years. I've seen you at services, and you've never cast a spell?" Marjory said.

"I'm hungry. Does anyone want me to go out for bread and eggs? I could make us all omelets and toast," Hiram said as he left the room.

The women followed after Hiram in a rush. The High Priestess caught Hiram just before he came to the grey garment that was still on the floor of the main room.

"Hiram what's going on?" Marjory said taking him by the arm and stopping him. "How is it you have never cast a spell. I really can't believe that is possible. I remember twenty years ago when there were still some women in The Church who might openly object to a man being a priest, but those were very old women. No one today is going to hold anything against you for doing this. Last year alone forty eight men were ordained here in Las Rotavas, at the university, not even mentioning those who took vows at Ses Theeth or other missions across the peninsula. What is the matter with you?"

"I don't know if I can do it," Hiram said dropping his head.

The Captain and Tiranna moved to encircle Hiram.

The Captain said, "Don't be absurd Hiram. You have one of the most gifted minds for organization and memory we have ever known."

"You repeated me word for word last night in the bathroom," Tiranna added and the other two women looked at her suspiciously.

"I was teaching him how to use the plumbing," Tiranna said shaking her head in disbelief.

"Right, right" Marjory said. "Hiram, there isn't any reason for you to doubt yourself. The spells, you know the spells you yourself classified as first level, at not very complicated. I'm sure you can do them."

"I have no rhythm," Hiram announced flatly.

"You have no rhythm? What do you mean you have no rhythm?" The Captain asked. "Hiram, you were given dancing lessons. You danced with me at the party, briefly yes, but you danced."

"I was following you!" Hiram exclaimed. "I could never dance on my own. When I listen to music I can't feel the rhythm. I can't follow the beat. Casting divine spells, in accordance with the doctrine of The Church, requires the spells to be canted, sung, you have to keep perfect time and rhythm. I can't do it."

"You can learn," the Captain said.

"We only have a few days to teach you, but I believe anyone can cast if their heart is correct and they have studied and memorized the prayers," Marjory said as she went back to Hiram's room to get the blue spell book. When she came back into the main room she stopped and looked down at the floor near the rest of them.

"Why is that on the floor in the middle of the room, and what is it?" Marjory asked.

"There are too many things going on at one time," the Captain said. "That is a package dropped off this morning by a woman claiming to be the natural sister of Madame Dorchester. According to the sergeant this woman dropped this off saying it was an inheritance left to Hiram from Madame Dorchester."

"What did this woman look like?" Marjory asked Tiranna.

"She could have been her sister, her natural sister. She had a similar face, and she was about the same height and build. She seemed younger," Tiranna said. "I was cautious, didn't let her in the house, nor did I tell her Hiram was here. I let her believe that Hiram was not here, and that I would get the package to him. She told me she had spoken to you."

"I never spoke to any of Madame Dorchester's relatives. Was there anything else odd about her, not just her appearance, anything at all that seemed out of place?" Marjory asked. "Could this be our mystery woman from the night at the hospital? Are we dealing with a shape shifter, or magic-user with some interest in our mission?"

"A magic-user, of course!" Tiranna exclaimed, and then shot Hiram a stare to remind him not to make any comment about her using that phrase. "I fell asleep last night unnaturally. I mean I feel asleep when I don't see why I would have. I was sitting next to Hiram. He was lying in his bed and I was holding his hand. The door was open behind me. When I woke, the door was closed and locked. And when I went to the front door, when this woman arrived, it was also locked, and I remember I hadn't locked it."

Marjory counted off on her fingers as she named the spells, "Sleep, Lock, Disguise Self," three very common arcane spells of low power and difficulty. We could very possibly be dealing with a magic-user, an arcane caster, for some reason, but I can't image why any wizard would be interested in this matter."

"Were you able to learn anything about this mystery woman Tiranna?" The Captain asked.

"I questioned everyone in the hospital before I was released. I checked the university duty rosters and a list of all campus residents. No one admitted buying any potions or visiting Hiram's apartment that night. When I questioned the vendor, the dwarven wizard, he remembered the woman who bought the potion that very same day matched the description of the woman I saw that night. He said she gave her name as Laurel, no other name."

"The potion was meant for Hiram," the Captain said. "Who ever it was knew about the Eysturlun agent and that there was a threat of poison. This person may be a wizard. A magic-user," she said the words with some disgust, "but whoever it is they obviously do not mean to harm Hiram, or you Tiranna, and they are trying to help in some small way."

"Do you think this item is some sort of protection, some enchanted item to help Hiram in some way?" Tiranna asked.

"There is a good, and easy, way to find out," Marjory said holding up the blue prayer book. "I haven't prepared spells this morning myself. I rushed out as soon as I got the message from the reverend mother. Hiram," she said firmly placing the book in Hiram's hand. "Go in your bedroom, go out on the veranda if you need to and study the spells for detecting evil, and detecting magic. Recite the prayers and when you are ready to try, come and get us we will be in the kitchen. The Captain and I have much to discuss. And with the Captain's approval maybe we can ask Tiranna to get us all something to eat. If there are any café's nearby."

"There is a shop right down the street that sells pastries stuffed with peppers, or eggs and tomatoes. I'll get us each a couple of them and be back right away. I want to see this accidental cleric cast his first spell," Tiranna said and left the apartment with a grin from ear to ear.

Part 25

Hiram took the prayer book and left the main room
without saying a word. Tiranna's comment hit him
like a brick. Was he just an accidental cleric? How
many people knew the truth about how he came to
be a priest? How many knew and never spoke about
it? He asked himself, "Was all the education and
dedication simply for show? Did he really never
consider that as a priest he would have to, someday,
cast a divine spell?"

His heart pounded in his chest as he walked out
onto the veranda. His paper on the classification and
order of divine magic, written when he was in his
second year, had been read before the Collective,
the body of women, all mothers, who make all of
the policies and set all of the practices for The
Church at Ses Theeth. On the campus even the
reverend mother had expressed some concern about
the radical paper. He would never know how close
he came to actually being accused of heresy, but the
word was used, and more than once.

He missed Madame Dorchester. She had died so
suddenly. They were as close as two people could
be and there were times when she was almost like a
mother to him. Madame Dorchester always spoke
with respect for the women of the Collective, and
the work they do, and now Hiram wondered if she
felt all of her life like Hiram was feeling now. Did
Madame Dorchester always wonder if she could

have become a priestess? Be nominated to the Collective, she was a mother after all? Did she feel she didn't do enough? Did she feel as though she mattered? Hiram felt like he was close, but not close enough to mattering. He was always being told these things, about his talents, his memory, his knowledge, but deep inside he knew he was not a real priest, he was just like Tiranna said, just an accidental cleric.

And why did she make him feel so confused about other things as well. He tried and he tried to be nice to her. He couldn't help it if he thought she was attractive. She was very pretty, even if she did look very young. Captain rower was a beautiful woman as well, and the High Priestess was probably one of the most attractive women he had ever seen in his life, but they didn't affect him the way Tiranna did.

Every time they were in the same room it was like he couldn't look at anyone else. She was smart mouthed, often rude, and had no patience with anyone. He could remember when he was holding her up in his bed that night she was hurt, how she smelled. When ever he let himself think about her, like now, his mind drifted into conflicting ideas and dream like conversations. Why was he feeling so attracted to her when at the same time he suspected how she hated him?

Holding the blue prayer book in his hands he began to wonder if he could actually do it, if he could actually cast a spell.

And why not?

He had mastered more areas of history, and general knowledge than anyone he had ever read about. He wasn't egotistical about it. He simple knew what he knew, and he knew that he knew a lot. He could master the sense of rhythm that he needed. It had to be possible. If he applied himself as thoroughly as he did when he wrote the paper that now was the standard for all clerics in The Church. He had to be able to do it. How hard could it be?

He walked to the edge of the veranda. The railing, a smooth wooden cap on a very thin brick and clay wall, felt warm as he put one hand on it. Hiram looked out across the beach and at the rolling breakers coming into the shore. There were a few small sailboats and a few people lying on the beach enjoying the warmth of the morning. The people looked peaceful. They looked as though they hadn't a care in the world. Hiram wanted to feel that, that feeling of serenity, and peace. He didn't need to show Tiranna he was capable, he didn't need to prove to them that he was everything they believed he was.

He opened the prayer book and began reading from the first page. Normally he would scan a book like this, find the relevant parts, and commit those to memory. This book meant more to him than that. He agreed to do this thing, this mission for The Church. He had never been asked to do anything that seemed as serious as this in his whole life. He remembered the time his parents had asked him if he wanted to stay in Liegridan, go to a mission school and eventually university. They had asked him if he really wanted to be a man of The Church at Ses Theeth, and he had said yes. They asked him if he was afraid, or if he would miss his family, and he remembered that what he said then, only twelve years old, was that he was not afraid and that he would miss them all, except his older sister because she was always mean to him. His parents had laughed and told him that he would probably find that he missed her too.

He missed her. He wanted to go to his sister's side and be with her. He wanted to show his sister that he could be as good a brother as he was anything else. He didn't need to prove he was a good cleric, but he needed to prove to himself, and to everyone else, that he was not just an accidental cleric.

End of Book I

Made in the USA
Lexington, KY
10 February 2012